Susie's Shoesies...

The Show Must Go On!

9/20/12

Trick-or-Treat to end
world hunger!

Sue Levine

Sue Madway Levine, Ed. D.

For information, address
THINGAMAJIG, INC.
PO Box 241, Mendenhall, PA 19357

ISBN-10: 0615620574
EAN-13: 9780615620572

Other books in the Susie's Shoesies series

Susie's Shoesies...Some Dreams Really Do Come True!

Olympic Dreams...Another Susie's Shoesies Adventure!

Susie's Shoesies...A Splendid Reward!

Look for the next exciting time-travel adventure,

Susie's Shoesies...The Mystery inside the Mystery!
coming to book stores in June 2013

Dedication

To the wonderful Academy In Manayunk school community; you are all wise beyond your years!

What Kind of Dream Is This?

The heat was oppressive; the sweat trickled down his cheek, and his drenched clothes stuck to his skin. And even though Owen was deep in slumber, as his body seemed to shift and sway, the bumpy road he was dreaming about became more and more real. With another huge jolt, he inhaled a breath of the dusty, hot air and experienced a suffocating sensation.

A moment later, Owen sensed he was tumbling into a hole; he panicked, opened his eyes, and was shocked to find his friend Bennett Gardner practically lying on top of him.

As he glanced around, all Owen could see were red dirt and a sky that looked like a rippling sea of dusty water, undulating under the scorching rays of the sun. It was then he noticed that he and his friends Bennett and Susie were in the middle of a huge, open-air, dilapidated truck, along with many other people he had never seen before. The truck leaned precariously to one side, which had caused the passengers to fall into each other.

Suddenly, three men who were dressed in brown, sweat-stained, shabby uniforms, with bandanas covering their faces, and rifles in their hands, came to the back of the truck and yelled in demanding and hostile voices to the passengers. Although they spoke a language Owen could not understand, there was something familiar about the words he could distinguish. When the other riders began to climb out of the vehicle, it was obvious the three friends from Merion, Pennsylvania, needed to follow their lead. And do so quickly.

Once he was safely on the ground, Owen's skin felt like it was on fire; without the slight breeze from the truck's movement along the road, there was no escaping the oven-like feeling that surrounded him.

When one of the drivers shouted and aimed his rifle at the group who had fled the truck, all the male passengers stepped forward. They surrounded the vehicle and, following more commands, grabbed the frame of the truck and began to lift and push it out of a deep rut.

Owen noticed the armed men and other passengers had the same dark skin as he had. His mind flashed back to the many photos of his family back in their homeland and to conversations his parents had with his grandparents and aunts and uncles, once they were all settled in Philadelphia.

An elderly woman approached Owen. She wore no more than a piece of colorful, striped fabric draped around her large frame, with another piece of the same cloth forming a coiled headscarf that wrapped around her hair. She put her arm around his shoulder and said, "Do not worry young man; the soldiers like to push us around so we will be too afraid to speak or try to get away. They know people are waiting for us and our tribal leader to arrive from our relocation camp. The show will not go on until we are there. But first, we must get this truck back on the road."

Susie leaned over and whispered to Owen, "What show? Where are we?"

The old woman pointed to Susie and Bennett and asked Owen, "Do you know these young people?" It seemed she had no idea where the children had come from any more than they knew how they had arrived at this remote, desert-like location.

Susie took it upon herself to answer the woman's question. "We are all friends at Merion Elementary School. Could you please tell us where we are?"

"I have never heard of such a school here in Somalia," the woman replied.

Without thinking, Owen shouted, "Somalia! What is going on? What show are you talking about? We don't go to school in Africa; we live in the United States!"

Susie and Bennett looked at each other with knowing eyes. They already had suspicions about what might be happening to them, but before they said another word, the old woman put her finger to her lips and quietly said, "Please, children. Do not speak again. It would not be wise to let the rebels know there are foreigners traveling with us. We are very lucky to have this chance to pick up water, food supplies, and the medicines we need to keep our families alive back at the camp. And we are all so hopeful to meet your American movie star who is letting the world know about the troubles we are having. Between the drought and famine, you would think our nation had enough problems. But mostly, we still fear the rival clans will be the death of us all!"

"Why do you live in a relocation camp? Where did these rebels come from, and why are they being so mean to all of you?" Susie asked.

Quietly, ever so quietly, the woman whispered, "It must have been around 1960 when England gave our country its independence. Many of us feared we were not ready for this new responsibility and that there were worse times yet to come. When our president was assassinated nine years later and the military took control, the new president backed the rebels and plunged our country into a civil war. It is thirty years later, and we are still a warring land. We have almost no running water, no electricity, and no way to grow crops, especially in the most southern region of our country. And our poor children do not seem to have much of a future, as there are so few schools for them to go to and better themselves."

Owen turned to Bennett and whispered, "Thirty years later? Is she saying it's 1990?"

As Bennett and Susie tried to piece together what was happening, the woman said, "But now that there are some famous people making our troubles known around the world, we have hope for the first time in many years. And if this truck can get us to Mogadishu and then on to Bidoa, we may get to see your Miss Hepburn and gather the courage to go on."

Owen could not believe what he was hearing. The three of them had learned a lot about Audrey Hepburn after their school science fair last December; Susie's mom had given her a special birthday gift... a copy of the book Miss Hepburn's son had written about his mother. Susie read to Bennett and Owen the part about the actress being named a *UNICEF* special ambassador in March 1988, after years of trying to help end world hunger.

During the next nine months, Owen spent a lot of time researching the life of the amazing actress, as well as starvation issues around the world. And it was just last night, at least Owen thought it was last night, when he had asked Susie to once again read certain sections from her book as background for his student government project. And now look what had happened!

"Bennett...Susie..." Owen turned to his friends and whispered, "Do you think we are going to meet Audrey Hepburn? How could this be? Didn't we read she died in 1993? This is 2009! No way could this be happening! Am I dreaming, or are we really in Africa?"

Susie put her arm around both boys as the truck was finally settled on even ground. The soldiers pushed everyone to the back of the vehicle as she whispered to Bennett, "Do you want to explain this to Owen or should I?"

CHAPTER ONE

A Tough School Year for Owen

Winning second place in the third-grade science fair last fall was a great achievement for Bennett and Owen. Many of their friends and classmates now wore sunglasses to school and on the ball field, and not just to look cool; their project on the harmful effects of sunlight had made quite an impression on everyone.

As the third-grade representative to the student government, Bennett's last school year had also been filled with numerous exciting and interesting opportunities, including the campaign to get every student in the school to sign the new anti-bullying pledge. There was a noticeable change in the hallways and sports fields at Merion Elementary School; there was less tension in the air, and the students seemed happier and more carefree. And for most of the children, it was easier to focus on important classroom projects and assignments. But not everyone was having such an easy time.

Now, in the fall of 2009, it was Owen's turn to make a difference at their school. He was the newly elected fourth-grade student government rep and had some ideas about a special project he wanted to champion. With a sense of well-being settling over his school, Owen wanted to look outside the walls of his own life, to try to make a larger contribution to his community. He sensed an obligation to pay-it-forward and help others who did not have the opportunities he and his school friends did.

Thanks to Susie's birthday present, Owen had become passionate about finding a way for his school to get involved in an effort to help starving children in Africa. And almost a year later, he was reading all he could about the history of Somalia, his native homeland, and the way different charities had gotten involved in the plight of that poor nation. Owen was especially interested in learning how one American actress could shine a light on the situation and help change the destiny of so many children.

On the Internet, Owen found what was called an 'interview transcript' from Audrey Hepburn's November 5, 1992, appearance on *The MacNeil/Lehrer NewsHour*, just after she returned to America from Somalia. When she was asked about what she saw there, the actress told the reporters how horrible the situation was. She described in shocking detail what it was like to watch young children die right in front of her eyes. She found that starvation and malnutrition themselves did not take most of the children's young lives; it was the illnesses their frail bodies were suscep-tible to *because* of the starvation that did.

Later in the conversation, Miss Hepburn talked about going to the town of Kismayo and how, as she walked around, she did not see any small children. She thought the children had been moved or taken to a hospital, but when she asked the villagers where they were, she was told they were all dead.

The actress went on to describe something that had happened in the town of Bidoa, known as a 'feeding center'. She explained this was a place where the children in the worst, possible shape were treated... children who were too weak to eat or drink.

Apparently, there was a malnourished little boy who was so thin and frail, all Miss Hepburn could see were his bulging eyes and bones. He wore just a scrap of fabric draped around his tiny frame. The young child struggled to breathe and, as she watched him suffer, she wished she could somehow breathe for him. Then he stopped trying, and life left his small body.

As if that weren't enough, when Owen found her fan website, _www.audrey1.org_, he read that she reportedly described Somalia as "apocalyptic". The website explained how she had visited several nations in Africa, including Ethiopia and Bangladesh, but found the circumstances in Somalia far worse than she ever could have imagined. Owen was moved to tears when he read how she described the situation as being nearly impossible to speak about, as it really was "unspeakable".

Owen's head was spinning and his heart was broken for his homeland, but he kept going. All of a sudden, he found some important and surprising information about the number of children who were starving in his adoptive country of America. He was shocked to learn that as many as seventeen million children in the United States struggled with what was called 'food insecurity'. That meant one out of every four children in America lived without a dependable source of food and the nutrition necessary to live a healthy life.

He dug further into the research about starvation in America. Owen wanted to learn more about what happened to children who did not eat a healthy diet, believing there had to be serious side effects from malnutrition. What he found actually scared him. Apparently, the brains of these starving children could be permanently scarred and cause them to have many different types of learning problems. These children also had more difficulty getting along with people and were more susceptible to frequent illnesses, which then caused them to miss important days of school.

One of the most frustrating things Owen learned was that although almost twenty million children were eligible to get a free or reduced lunch at school, only ten million got a free or reduced breakfast. That meant over ten million others started their school days with empty stomachs. What was even worse was that most of the children who got their breakfasts and lunches at school could not do so during the summer months when their schools were closed. At best, they ate one meal a day, and often woke up hungry and went to bed just as hungry.

There was a personal side to the research Owen was completing. Last spring, his teacher and parents asked him to meet with Dr. Roberts, the school psychologist at Merion Elementary, to complete some tests and find out why he was falling behind in his reading and writing skills. Now, in the fall of his fourth-grade year, Owen felt his problems were only getting worse. Although the testing supposedly determined he was very smart, the findings also indicated he had difficulty concentrating and remembering what he read, and his spelling and handwriting skills were also below grade level.

Owen could read almost everything he wanted to, but once he reached the bottom of a page, sometimes he could not remember what he had just finished. And even though he could accurately read the words in his textbooks, many did not make sense to him. His teacher, Mrs. Blair, explained to him that reading was "a search for meaning," not just being able to say the words on a page.

When he was working on the research for his science fair project in the University of Pennsylvania library, he had to keep asking his friends what words like 'autobiographical' and 'radiation' meant. It was so frustrating to be able to read the words as easily as Susie and Bennett could, but not make sense of them the way they did with ease.

As he researched world hunger, he wondered if having lived in a starving country like Somalia during the first few years of his life may have affected his own brain development. No one could give him a definite answer as to what may have caused his learning issues, but the school did find him a patient and helpful tutor to try and keep his schoolwork on track. She was teaching him some important strategies to help him understand and remember what he read.

One of the things Owen's tutor had him practice was 'visualizing'. He could remember Mrs. Blair often said, "Good readers visualize; when they read or listen to someone speak, it's like they are playing a movie in their heads. If they are reading about a cold and windy day, they can see people shivering as they walk down the street, pulling their coats tight as the wind moves them along."

This skill did not come naturally to Owen, and it was not easy for him to do. So his tutor taught him to listen and try to see the colors, sizes, and shapes associated with the words he read or heard.

Even though Dr. Roberts had told him none of these problems meant he was not smart enough to do well in school (apparently, intelligence had nothing to do with it), what he was most afraid of was that his friends might not understand this and think less of him when he could not answer his teachers' questions.

Owen was a leader in his class and had many close friends... especially Bennett and Susie Gardner. But deep within his heart, he wondered if his other friends would stand by him when he kept making embarrassing mistakes in class.

Like his tutor, Owen's mother was patient with him and seemed to understand his issues and concerns. She was always available for help with his assignments and tried to comfort and reassure him when his learning problems surfaced. However, during class discussions and questions, he kept his head down and did not look at his teacher, for fear of being called on for an answer. And even though he could usually read through literature and his textbook passages with ease, he never volunteered to read out loud in class for the same reason.

More and more, he was getting less and less out of school. His mother told him it was his fear of making a mistake that actually caused him to be less able to pay attention to the meanings behind the words he read. She thought those fears were distractions that took him off in another direction...and Owen was beginning to believe her.

CHAPTER TWO

Where Did I Come From?

"Mom, can I talk to you and Dad about something serious?" Owen asked. "Remember when you told me you thought my worries about my schoolwork were getting in the way of my learning? Well, I do think you were right about that, but it may be worse than you imagined."

Owen had just sat down at the dinner table with his parents and his five-year-old sister Katie when he began the meal with this unsettling comment. Limpho and Baruti Kane knew their son was under a lot of pressure at school, but thought things were improving. This sounded like a setback.

Baruti reached across the table and grasped Owen's right hand between both of his own. "What is it, my son? What has you so upset? Your mother told me you were doing much better in school. Tell me why you look so sad, and how we can help you."

"Oh, Dad, I have been researching the history of Somalia. Remember that movie I told you about last fall, the one I saw when I stayed over at Bennett's house for his sister's birthday...around the time of the

7

fall science fair? It was about a famous actress, Audrey Hepburn, who tried to help the people from our country."

"I remember, my son. I am proud that you want to know more about our native homeland. But what does this have to do with getting your schoolwork done? Is this new project taking too much time away from your studies?"

"Not at all. I am so focused; in fact, none of my concentration or word problems are getting in the way of this work at all. It is amazing how much I am learning and remembering," Owen reported.

He had wondered how he could recall the batting average of every one of the Phillies' ballplayers if he had such significant memory problems. And now, this project he dedicated so much of his time to had led to a huge amount of knowledge he never would have thought he could understand.

He had spoken with Dr. Roberts about this, wondering if maybe his learning issues were cured. She told him that many students who were distractible and had trouble concentrating were able to hyper-focus on things that were especially important and meaningful to them.

Between the help he got from his tutor and the research he was doing for his hunger project, Owen was beginning to feel proud and hopeful about his schoolwork, and wanted to let his father know how passionate he felt about what he was learning.

"So, after watching that movie and reading more about Somalia, when I got elected to the student government last spring, I wanted to plan an event at school to raise money for a charity that helps the starving people in Africa. It is unbelievable to me that our family came from a country that is still in so much trouble. But what I have found out now is just as upsetting. Did you know there are millions of children in America who are also starving? What is going on in the world? How can there be so much hunger and starvation right here in the United States? Is that why we left Africa? Were we starving? Please tell me...it is important that I know everything about our life there."

Owen's parents knew there would come a day when their children would ask these difficult questions. But they were not prepared for the conversation to begin at the dinner table that evening.

Limpho spoke up and said, "My darling children, yes...that is why we left Mogadishu."

"But Mom, were we starving? I have been reading a lot about the effects of starvation on the brain. It can cause all kinds of learning problems. Is that what is wrong with me? Was my brain damaged because of the conditions we lived in?"

As soon as those words came out of Owen's mouth, his younger sister began to cry. "Is my brain damaged too?" Katie asked.

Their mother answered first. "No, my little one; there is nothing wrong with your brain. The situation here in America today is very different from what was happening in Africa back in 2004, but that does not mean the current suffering in our country is less harmful. Your father and I are aware of the plight of the poor and homeless people in our new homeland, and you know we have been active in our church's efforts to help keep the Food Cupboard full and flowing with essentials for the hungry in our own community."

Owen noticed she made no comment about *his* brain. He decided to let that go for the moment. "And that's the point, Mom; I want our school and the other schools in our district to get more involved in helping others. We have to…we are so lucky to have the blessings that have come our way. We must pay back what has been given to us," he said. "I have found a lot of information I can use for this project, but our family's own story might help my friends at school feel the pain that others have to live with on a daily basis."

"A personal perspective is always helpful, son," Baruti replied. "Maybe we should back up a bit. Let me tell you a little of the history you may not yet have read about. But son, don't be afraid to jump in and add to what I am going to tell you and your sister. I have a feeling you may remember more than I do about some of the issues we should talk about."

It made Owen proud to know his father respected his opinion. Maybe, just maybe, his family's experience would make the difference between a successful project and one that went nowhere. At the same time, he was also looking for information that other people's research could not give him…answers to why he had so much trouble with his studies.

As Baruti looked over at his young daughter, he could see she was worried. "Katie, do not look so sad," he said. "There is much for you to feel proud of when you consider what your grandparents and your mother and I have been through. Listen as I tell you the story of our homeland." He picked her up and held her on his lap as he began to tell the story of their lives in Somalia and journey to America.

"Because of its location on the Indian Ocean, before the year 1000, Somalia was used as a coastal trading post by the Arabs and Persians. Over the next centuries, many different people, such as the Turks,

Italians, French, and British, controlled our land. But when we were given our independence in 1960, we did not know what to expect. Your mother and I came from the same small village and were youngsters at the time, just about two years old, right, Limpho? Like everyone else, even though we were so little, we could sense the tension in the air and see the signs of concern on the faces of our families…and I remember feeling afraid of things I did not understand and that were happening all around us."

"Our new nation's first president, Abdirashid Ali Shermarke, was assassinated by one of his body-guards in 1969, and a new president, Major General Muhammad Siad Barre, took power the day of Shermarke's funeral. At first, it seemed like Somalia could become the model nation for democracy in Africa. Siad Barre organized a labor force that planted and harvested crops, built roads and hospitals, and created a new written language. Yes, by the time I was about ten or eleven years old, I felt like the tide might be turning in the right direction."

"In 1974, when I was sixteen, President Siad Barre took more than twenty thousand students out of their secondary schools to travel to the rural areas of the land and attempt to educate their relatives. I was one of those students, and that is when my family changed my name to 'Baruti' which, as you know, means 'educator'."

"Then what happened?" Owen asked.

"Unfortunately, it was not long before Siad Barre decided to develop ties with Russia and, within a year, various clans had been armed and were fighting our own people for control of the land. Before we knew it, our country went to war with Ethiopia in the late

1970s. We were defeated and what followed were more years of political unrest and civil war. None of the supplies the international community sent got through to us. When Siad Barre finally fled Somalia in 1991, the guerilla warriors were in control."

"How did you survive, Mom?" Owen asked.

"It was very difficult, my darling," Limpho said, as she reached over to put her arm around her son. "There were charities that air-dropped grain and medical supplies, but often the soldiers got to them before the villagers could."

"One day, I was tending a small patch of land by the side of our hut where my mother had planted some beans, corn, and squash, when I heard the planes overhead," Limpho said. "All of a sudden, I saw three enormous wooden pallets dropping from the sky, near to where I was standing. When they hit the red earth, a huge cloud of dust rose up and covered my face and body. I called for my father and he, along with some of the other villagers...including the tall and handsome man who is now your father...ran over to see what was in the burlap bags tied to the wooden planks. What we saw amazed us. There were bags of wheat flour, rice, dried corn meal, and many different kinds of medical supplies too. We believed they were gifts from god, and that is when my family renamed me 'Limpho', which means 'gift' in Somali."

"We quickly covered the materials with blankets and straw to keep the soldiers from finding them. Our village was so desperate for supplies. We decided to use one-third of our daily water rations to grow additional crops. But besides the needed supplies, another gift was coming to our family in particular; Baruti and I were making plans to get married!"

"Although we were able to take pleasure in the happy moments, it was still a terrible time for all of us," Baruti added. "Many years of peace negotiations had led to only small changes because there was so much political corruption. Our food supplies were gone and even our hospitals were destroyed; the guerillas stole everything in sight."

"But in 1992, there was a final truce and it was then the United States sent not only food and supplies but also soldiers to help make sure they reached the people of Somalia."

"When the northern part of our country declared its independence and the world recognized it as 'Puntland', the southern part of Somalia, where our families lived, was still under the control of the rebels. But things were not as dangerous as they had been, and we had hope for the future."

"'Puntland' is such a funny name, Dad. Why did they call it that?" Katie asked.

"What a good question, my little one. The 'Land of Punt' is mentioned in ancient Egyptian writings. No one knew exactly where it was located, but in 1998, during an important meeting in Garowe, the elite leaders of the new nation decided to take that name," Baruti told her.

"It sounds like things were getting better, Mom," Owen said. "So why did you and our grandparents decide to leave?"

"Yes, things were better, but far from perfect," Limpho said. "By this time, your father and I had married and were hopeful the country's recovery would continue. Although many of the rebels had been disarmed and Somalia was beginning to recover, by the turn of the century, there was still political unrest. In

2000, Owen, you were born, and all we could think about was keeping you strong and healthy. And then came the December 24, 2004, Asian tsunami and the resulting mass destruction of lives and homes all along the east coast of Africa. We lost many members of our extended family."

Their father continued, "When we found out your mother was pregnant with you, Katie, we began to think about leaving our homeland. By now I was a well-respected professor in Africa, and when the tsunami struck and the international aid rallied to help people from all the affected nations, we took this as an opportunity to do what we and your grandparents had to do in order to survive. All four of my brothers had been killed in either the civil unrest or the tsunami; we knew if we wanted a future for our family, we would have to leave. We left with a military aid group from Pennsylvania, and here we are today."

"What about Miss Hepburn, Dad? Did you get to meet her in 1992, when she spoke in Somalia? Did you know that she was very sick and died the next year?" Owen asked.

"Actually, my son, I almost did get to see her. It was the year before your mother and I married. One day, some of the remaining rebels brought a truck to our village and rounded us all up in the back of their vehicle. Do you remember, Limpho, how hot it was that day, and how mean they were to our village elders?"

"Yes, I do, my dear," she replied.

"They drove us about three hours, to a relocation camp in the middle of the desert filled with, oh, maybe a thousand people...and then chose some of our villagers to travel ahead to Bidoa and what we later found out was an event offered by the *United Nations Children's Fund...UNICEF.*"

"Your mother and I were not allowed to go; there wasn't enough room on the truck. But when our people returned, they had new hope in their hearts. As it turned out, they had seen Miss Hepburn. It was only after we came to America that we realized all the amazing sacrifices this wonderful actress and humanitarian had made for our people," Baruti said.

"But getting back to your earlier questions regarding your brain development and learning problems, Owen; in our village, whatever food we had was always given to the children and pregnant mothers. We knew our country's hopes for the future were in their precious hands and we provided them with everything we could. They ate first and more than the rest of us. Was it enough? I am quite sure it was not. So yes, there is a chance that during the first four years of your life, you did not have all the essential things needed to make you as strong and healthy as you could be."

"Katie, you were born here in America, six months after we got to this country; we gave your mother all that we could while she was pregnant and once we had made our way to our new homeland, we no longer feared for her or our family's well-being," Baruti said.

"Owen, we did everything we could to take care of you and your sister. And when I look at you, Mister fourth-grade representative to the student government, I know it was enough to make you the son we are so proud of. Did you know that our American family name, 'Kane', came from your Somali first name 'Kefentse', which means 'conqueror'? When we entered America in 2004, and wrote your name on the immigration papers, the authorities misread what we wrote and listed 'Kane' as our family name. In a way, it is quite fitting, don't you think? Our family and people have overcome and conquered all obstacles put before us. And you will continue in that tradition, my son. Of that, I have no fear."

CHAPTER THREE

Susie Tells Owen

The shouting and pushing were beyond frightening. Guns waving, shots firing, children crying; the soldiers' efforts to get the villagers back on the truck were a nightmare. The older woman who had befriended Susie, Bennett, and Owen gathered them close to her side, in order to shield them from the eyes of the rebels.

As one elderly man tried to step up into the truck, he fell to the ground. The tallest and meanest of the clansmen hit him on the head with the butt of his rifle, and then two others dragged him over to the rut on the side of the road and shoved him in. This only led to more crying and yelling as the villagers knew he would surely die if left alone in the desert.

"We've got to help him!" Owen said to the old woman, who seemed to be a leader among her people.

"You must be quiet, my child. And you cannot be heard speaking your English language. It could bring harm to all of us. When we get to Mogadishu, we will tell the others where he is and perhaps then they can come to his rescue," she replied. "He is the brother of my father, and I will not let him die like an animal, even though the rebels treat all of us like we are."

"They are the ones who are behaving like animals," Susie said. "They are just bullies and we know all about people who pick on others, don't we guys?"

"You are right, my child. The only people who do not understand their behavior are the rebels themselves. You see, there is no work for these young men and, because they get food and shelter from their clan leaders, they have chosen violence as their professions. They know nothing else. Their families have all been murdered so they have no one but each other. Power is what they crave, even power over innocent and peaceful people, like those from my village. But they are most foolish to underestimate us as we are not fools. We may be old and tired and hungry, but we are also patient and will wait for our time and place to take back our lives. They will never take our spirit or our love for the country we used to know."

Susie and the boys were amazed by the courage and conviction of this woman and her villagers. As they took their seats in what space they could find on the floor of the dusty truck, the tailgate slammed shut and Owen turned to Bennett and whispered, "What were you two going to tell me? Do you understand what is going on? Do you guys know how we got here? None of this makes any sense to me!"

Susie decided to tell Owen the mysterious truth… a truth that defied imagination. Quietly, she began. "Well, Owen, remember the research you were doing for your student government project on feeding the hungry…and you asked me to read you some of the information from the book my mother gave me last December for my ninth birthday? Think back for a moment; what is the last thing you remember before we found ourselves here in Africa?"

"I was sleeping over at your house. We were all going to bed in Bennett's room, and you had your book in your hand; you were going over the part about Audrey Hepburn's work in Somalia...the part I asked you to read to us again. One of the last things I remember is telling you what I had learned about the millions of children starving right here in America."

"Did you notice anything unusual while we were talking?" Bennett asked his friend.

"Well, I remember we had turned out the lights, but we were able to see each other and you could read to us, Susie, because of a bright red glow in the room," Owen replied. "Now that we're talking about this, I remember wondering where that light was coming from."

He looked down to where he and his friends were huddled together in the truck. It was then he noticed Susie's birthday shoes. And, in the dusty shadows beneath all the legs and other feet that surrounded them, those shoes seemed to be glowing!

"You know what, Susie? I am looking at your shoes right now...and honestly...they look like they have a light inside of them. Are you saying you were wearing them at bedtime, while you were reading to us? Did they make the red light I saw in Bennett's room?" Owen asked. "What are they, some kind of magical time machine?"

"Well, that was easier than I thought it would be," Bennett said to his sister.

"What are you saying? That's it? They really are magical?" Owen shouted.

"Shhhh," Susie cautioned him. "Not so loud. We have to be careful. But the short answer is...yes, they appear to possess some kind of magical ability...they have either caused Bennett and me to have the exact same dreams at the exact same time, or have allowed us to really travel back to the past. We don't know which of these possibilities is more impossible to believe."

Susie went on to tell Owen how her great-great-grandmother, Didi, bought the shoes from a *shaman* in Russia for her first granddaughter, Susie's Granny Ella, when Ella turned eight years old.

"Oh, wait. Let me guess; then your grandmother Ella gave them to you on your eighth birthday! I know a lot about *shamans* and other mystics from some of the role playing games Bennett and I play. Cool...this is all very cool," Owen said, as he relaxed a little. "But they're not real, are they? This isn't really happening, is it? Pinch me."

Bennett leaned over and squeezed his friend's arm.

"I felt that; I felt that! Oh, no...we really are in Africa! How will we ever get home?" Owen asked.

CHAPTER FOUR

Are We There Yet?

As the open air truck slowly made its way along the hot and dusty road, the villagers and their unusual visitors dozed off from time to time. Susie thought there was something comforting about this large group of people who held each other near, even though they faced the uncertainty of the journey they were on.

The old woman who seemed to be protecting them had taken off her head scarf and covered the tops of their heads with it. She had noticed Susie and Bennett were getting sunburned and was concerned they might get so dizzy they would be unable to walk, if ordered to do so. That could lead to a disastrous result.

No one on the truck had had food or water in the hours since their trip began; many of the people groaned in their sleep as their stomachs ached and their mouths were too dry to swallow. But there were no complaints. The villagers would not give the rebels the satisfaction of knowing they suffered from their treatment.

Suddenly, the truck came to a screeching halt. The clansmen got out of the front of the vehicle and banged on its wooden sides to wake their weary captives. With a loud clang, the heavy tailgate came crashing down and the soldiers yelled at the villagers once again.

They had arrived at what looked and felt like a prison in the middle of the desert. Inside an enormous span of barbed-wire fencing stood a few crumbling wooden buildings and what appeared to be more than one thousand people who looked out at the new arrivals. Some people huddled under the few trees that grew in the compound, but the situation looked dire; how would they all survive the midday's sun without cover? As Susie looked at the dried and cracked lips of the captives behind the fence, she knew finding water would be essential.

When the villagers on the truck saw people they recognized behind the enclosure, they shouted out and ran toward them. There was no need for the guards to hurry them along.

Right away, the elderly woman who had befriended the children climbed down off the back of the truck and rushed over to one of the guards. When she shoved him so hard that he almost fell down, Susie and Bennett gasped in fear of what would happen next. But the woman was undaunted; she was outraged as she went on to exchange some very cross words with him...and then turned and walked back to her people who were still exiting the truck. The soldier hung his head in despair and looked like he might even be crying.

"What did you say to him?" Owen asked.

"I told him what they had done to his uncle! That is my brother, and he promised to send some of the men back to pick up our father's brother from where his evil friends had left him. You see, my children, in all the chaos that has surrounded our country, now, even after the worst of the violence is over, many of our young men no longer remember how to act like civilized and responsible members of our village. After my other two brothers died in the fighting, my only surviving brother, the man you saw me arguing with, was recruited by one of the most violent clan leaders. And for the past five years, he has known nothing else."

The children were relieved to think the old man they had left in the rut by the side of the road would survive his ordeal. It seemed like this woman was smart; she knew what needed to be done to take care of her people. Bennett turned and said, "Stay close to her; she has our backs and it seems like even the soldiers know not to mess with her."

Once they were inside the fence, several people rushed over to embrace the children and their protector. Although the children could not understand what the villagers said, they heard the word 'Kagiso' over and over.

"Maybe that's her name," Susie said to the boys.

"Well, there is one way to find out," Owen replied. He walked over to the woman who had sheltered them and said, "Thank you for helping us, Kagiso; we could not have made it through this without you."

"You are very welcome, my American child. Now you will have the protection of my entire village. We will let no harm come to you or your friends. You are our guests, just like your American actress, Audrey Hepburn."

Owen smiled for the first time in several hours; he would have to ask his father what the name 'Kagiso' meant when he got home...if he ever got home.

A large group of young children surrounded Susie and Bennett. Although Owen thought it might be the pair's fair skin that attracted the attention, he soon noticed it was the glow from Susie's shoes that fascinated them. All of a sudden, a little girl who stood outside the fence started pulling on one of the soldier's sleeves and pointing at Susie's feet. When Kagiso saw this happening, she leaned over to Susie and said, "Do not say a word; let me do all the talking, my child. The soldier who is moving toward us is the leader of this rebel clan and that is his daughter coming with him. He is a terrible man and I will try to calm him down."

The child rushed ahead of her father and ran right over to Susie. In a flash, she sat on the ground and began to try to take off Susie's shoes. Susie, Bennett and Owen were the only prisoners, if that is what they were, who wore shoes, and from the look of the little African girl's feet, she may never have even tried on a pair of shoes.

When Susie struggled with her, her soldier father fired his rifle into the air. Everyone nearby ran toward one of the wooden sheds to hide, except for Susie, Bennett, Owen, and Kagiso. Susie knew she had to let Kagiso handle this situation. As the rebel and Kagiso argued back and forth, the three Merion Elementary children stood huddled together, perfectly still.

The next thing that happened was such a shock to Susie that she thought she would faint. Kagiso bent down and took off her special shoes! In a defiant manner, she held her hand up to Susie's face as if to say, "Not a word; do not move or say a word."

As the soldier's daughter put on the shoes, she smiled at her father who then picked her up in his arms. He made one more apparently rude comment to the tribal elder and walked away with his child.

Susie was devastated. She felt like her world was coming to an end. Her granny's shoes were gone! She did not know whether to cry or scream, but Kagiso appeared to want her to keep quiet.

The shoes had been in her family for more than seventy-five years, but had only belonged to Susie for two; how could she have let this happen? This would surely break her grandmother's heart. And how would they ever get back to America without them?

When she watched the father and daughter leave through the guarded gate, Susie noticed the glow from her shoes became dimmer and dimmer. Although it surprised Owen, it did not surprise Susie or Bennett a bit. "That's what happens whenever I take them off, Owen. But I always wondered what would happen if someone else put them on."

Suddenly, a loud bell rang and all the villagers gathered along the side of the largest wooden building in the yard. Kagiso led Susie, Bennett, and Owen over to where her villagers had settled on the ground. As they took their seats among the other refugees, the three children wondered what was about to happen.

Susie noticed a large, scaled, brown bug climbing up her brother's leg. No, 'large' was not the right word; it was enormous. 'Disgusting' was a better word to describe the critter. Susie did not know what to do. If she screamed, it might scare Bennett and Owen to death. She was too afraid to touch the ugly thing herself and was considering knocking it off her brother's leg with a twig. But then she thought about the possibility of that bug crawling back up the stick and onto her own hand. Oh, what to do?

25

Kagiso noticed Susie seemed scared and upset. When she looked to where the young American's eyes were directed, the kind old woman calmly reached over and picked up the bug. "It will not harm your brother, dear child. I remember the first time I saw one on my arm; it frightened me so much and I screamed so loud, my father thought we were being attacked by a lion. The bug is called a 'cicada', and it may surprise you to know that they are quite delicious when they are as young as this one is."

To Susie's horror, Kagiso put the insect in her mouth and began to chew. "They have much nutrition, and when we are so very hungry, they are a gift from the sky."

Just when Susie began to realize how hungry she was, a large truck pulled into the yard. The tailgate was unlatched and the soldiers climbed out of the back, carrying what looked like large pots of hot cereal. The steaming containers were passed among the people; young and old alike simply reached into the nearest pot and took a handful of the unpleasant looking mixture. When Kagiso took her share, Susie and the boys reached in and did the same.

"You must eat, my children. You need your strength to continue on our journey."

"So, are we really going to see the American actress, Kagiso?" Owen asked.

"Yes, dear child. I think we only need to travel a little further till we get to Bidoa where they will have our show. Now eat up…and be sure to go over to the water pump and have a good long drink…but not too much or too fast or it might make you sick."

While everyone was eating, Owen spoke up. "What's going to happen to us, now that your shoes are gone? How will we ever get out of here?"

"When my granny gave me my shoes, she told me to be prepared to trust my heart. I am not sure what is going to happen in the end, but I have a feeling everything will work out just fine. Even though I am a little worried, I am not going to let it take away from this amazing opportunity. We are in your homeland and may be about to see Miss Hepburn! Think of what this can mean for your project!"

The excitement in Susie's voice encouraged Owen. Once he set his fears aside, he realized this could be a once in a lifetime chance to understand what his people had endured. With Susie not only walking without her shoes, but barefoot, Owen realized he was walking in the path of his ancestors.

CHAPTER FIVE

Good News from Above

Once again, a loud and steady noise frightened the villagers. Children started to cry and the elderly began to chant what seemed like a prayer or song. This time, even Kagiso looked concerned.

Susie thought the sound was coming from the sky; as she looked up and pointed, everyone around her did the same. Bennett turned to Owen and said, "Look...it's planes! And look at the letters on the tail!"

"Oh, my goodness!" cried Owen. "It's an American plane! Maybe it is carrying Miss Hepburn! Maybe it is bringing supplies for the people of Somalia...and maybe they will rescue us."

Susie exhaled and her body relaxed for the first time in hours. She finally had a clear picture of what was happening to them and the villagers. She turned to the boys and said, "Miss Hepburn died in 1993. But during the last year of her life, she traveled to Somalia...to bring attention to the problems of your homeland, Owen. It must be the fall of 1992, and it looks like you might get to see her after all!"

Kagiso moved over to Susie and asked her what the plane was doing. Many of the people from her village had never seen an airplane before and were afraid. Susie said, "I think it is bringing the great actress to see your people. And it might also mean that help is on the way."

Owen was the next to offer comfort to his people. "We read about this in a book Miss Hepburn's son wrote about his mother."

Suddenly Bennett pulled his friend aside. "Owen, we can't talk about what we read; for the villagers, this time in Somali history has not yet taken place; they would not understand how we know what is going to happen next. After all, even you don't understand how this is possible, do you?"

"Wow, that's a good point," Owen said. "But wait a minute; there are some things we had better warn them about. If we tell them about the tsunami that is coming in 2004, we could save so many lives. Maybe we should just tell Kagiso...she will know what to do."

"You know, Susie and I have talked about this a lot," Bennett told him. "This is not the first time we believe we have traveled back in time. There were other opportunities when we thought telling people about Susie's shoes and what history held in store for them could save lives. But we worried that if we changed one event, it could lead to even worse things to come. And anyway, who would believe us? Who believes in time travel?"

"Well, I do," said Owen. "I have to think about this some more. After all, these are my people. Some of them might even be my relatives. If I have a chance to save them, wouldn't it be worth the risk?"

At that moment, several trucks came through the gate, bringing with them another cloud of choking dust. This time, the soldiers did not have to tell their captives what to do; everyone climbed into the vehicles. Susie, Bennett, and Owen made sure they got on board.

There was not enough room for all the refugees to squeeze in; many were left behind. Owen looked back at the disappointed faces leaning up against the fence surrounding the compound and felt his heart skip a beat. Holding hands and looking desperate to leave the confinement of the camp were two people with familiar faces. As he looked into the eyes of the young man, Owen could see himself; and there was something about the mouth of the young woman by this villager's side that reminded him of his sister Katie. Suddenly, Owen felt such a pang of homesickness that he wanted to get off the truck and run to the young Somali couple.

"Bennett, look at that man and woman standing up against the fence near the gate! Who do they remind you of?" Owen asked. "I need to know who they are!"

Neither Bennett nor Susie heard him. The trucks had started to leave the detention camp with a thunderous roar, and Kagiso was trying to get the attention of her people. Owen and his friends could not understand what she was saying, but the villagers seemed happy with the news she gave them. They hugged each other and sang a song that sounded full of joy and hope. But Owen still had his doubts.

CHAPTER SIX

A Star in the Evening Sky

The sun was still painfully hot, but there was an excitement in the air that seemed to cool the weary villagers. The rebels were not as harsh as they had been earlier in the day, and with Kagiso's brother at the wheel, the three young American travelers were less apprehensive than before.

It took another two hours to arrive at what appeared to be their final destination. Everyone was exhausted from the heat of the day and the red dirt that seemed to coat not only the outside of their bodies, but deep inside their souls.

"My friends, we have arrived in what appears to be Bidoa," Kagiso said. "I have heard of this place...it is a feeding station. This is where your Miss Hepburn is supposed to put on her show. Oh, I pray this is a good thing and that supplies are coming."

As Susie, Bennett, and Owen looked around, the red dirt desert floor did not look very welcoming. It had been years since the beautiful American actress had starred in a live performance, and the trio did not remember reading in her son's biography about his mother performing in Somalia. Bennett turned to Owen and said, "I am worried the villagers will be upset if there is no show; they have already been through so much, and journeyed so far. How will they handle another disappointment?"

Susie replied, "As long as there are supplies, I think they will understand that this is no place to hold a play. Without electricity or even a platform for her to stand on, there is no possible way for Miss Hepburn to perform. Besides, remember how ill she is! It seems like it would be almost impossible for her to even show up."

As Bennett tried to see over the heads of the villagers, he found what he was looking for. "Look... over there, everyone. I see an American flag near that building! And isn't that the flag of the United Nations right next to it? And look at all the people in clean uniforms! No red desert dirt on them," Bennett pointed out to his friends.

Sure enough, Susie and Owen saw what Bennett did. "They're Americans and could rescue us, Susie," Owen whispered, afraid to think their ordeal might soon be over.

"Maybe they can, but I am not leaving until I get my granny's shoes back," Susie said in a determined tone. "Think about it, you guys; we don't want them to take us home; if they do, they will be taking us back to 1992. Trust me...I *will* get us home...home to the year 2009."

The villagers were led off the truck into yet another fenced-in area. There was no shouting or pushing this time, and it appeared the soldiers were trying to make a good impression for the international guests. This enclosure was smaller than where they were held near Mogadishu, and had more trees and buildings. But the conditions were still far from ideal. Kagiso kept an eye on her young friends and helped them find a place along the fence where they could watch the people who had started to move in their direction.

At first, there was no sign of the famous actress. Then all of a sudden, the sea of foreigners parted and there, among a group of important-looking men, stood one small woman in a dark t-shirt and what might have been jeans. She looked tired and frail, and there was a sadness that seemed to surround her still lovely face and caring eyes. She wore her hair pulled back in a bun, much like the way she did in her movies. There was no doubt who she was; this was Audrey Hepburn!

Of course Susie, Bennett, and Owen knew something very few people who were present at this historic occasion knew, and that was that Miss Hepburn was seriously ill. Owen turned to his friends and said, "You know what this means, don't you? She visited Somalia in September of 1992, and died less than a year later. How brave she is...she dedicated the final months of her life to helping other people."

Suddenly, the actress was out of sight. They rushed over to a nearby well and Bennett climbed on top to see what he could see. "There she is...walking among the villagers. Now she is kneeling down and holding one of the babies who looks like he is starving. She is really upset!"

"It is all so very sad, boys. So many of these people will die," Susie said. A tear ran down her cheek and she began to sob. Kagiso wrapped her in her strong arms and tried to comfort her.

For what seemed like an hour, the actress continued to make her way among the starving babies and villagers, surrounded by numerous people representing many different organizations. Of course, many of the visitors were wearing the *UNICEF* logo which made perfect sense, as the young Americans knew Miss Hepburn was their special ambassador. Susie noticed an older woman in a uniform with the name '*CARE*' on it. "Owen, have you done any research on an organization called '*CARE*'?" Susie asked.

Bennett was the next to make an important discovery. Inside the building near the well were bags and bags of what looked like supplies; some were marked with the label '*WHO*' while others had a large, red cross on the outside. "And add '*WHO*' to the list of organizations you need to find out about when we get home, Owen."

"You bet I will, assuming we do get home. You're sure about this getting back to Merion business, Susie?" Owen asked.

"Like my granny says, "trust your heart", and everything will work out in the end. But for us, the end will be knowing we have done something to help stop starvation." Susie added.

"Do you think our project could make a difference?" Owen asked.

"Just as soon as I get my shoes back, I know we will make Miss Hepburn proud. And speaking of her, where did she go?"

The children looked all around; they ran from one side of the fence to another, but the actress was nowhere in sight. In the distance, they heard the sound of a plane moving away from where they were standing.

"I think she is on her way," Susie said. "Oh, I wish we could have talked to her and told her how proud of her we are."

"I don't know. Maybe it's better this way. After all, in real life, Miss Hepburn never did get to meet us. It might have caused a problem as we tried to explain how we got to Somalia. It could have confused her or even upset her, and she probably had enough on her mind," Bennett suggested.

Suddenly, in a sad and disappointed voice, Kagiso said, "But there has been no show...we thought we were going to see your American star in a show."

"But Kagiso, we did get to see a show, just not the kind you and your people were expecting. This was a show of courage! Did you notice how thin and tired-looking Miss Hepburn was? The truth is, she is very..." Susie stopped herself, realizing she could not go any further without having to explain how she, Bennett, and Owen had gotten to Somalia and how they knew so much about the great actress.

Susie looked up at Owen and said, "You know, you can't tell anyone we were here. First of all, no one would believe us, and second of all, we have to keep the story of my shoes a secret. And speaking of my shoes," she added, "I think I know how this will all work out. Believe me; I will be wearing my granny's birthday present by tomorrow."

CHAPTER SEVEN

Who's Afraid of the Dark?

As soon as things had calmed down, the villagers began roaming through the enclosure, gathering up piles of hay that were stacked in bundles around the dilapidated building. "Come with me, little ones," Kagiso said. "We need to make a soft place for us to rest our heads when we sleep tonight. Each of you take as much hay as you can carry. I am not sure if the rebels will be feeding us, but in any case, if we stay together, we can count on my brother to keep us safe."

Bennett turned to his sister and said, "So it looks like we won't be going home so soon. Do you still think we have nothing to worry about?"

"The fact that it is getting dark is a good thing, boys. Try not to be afraid," Susie said in her most reassuring voice. "Think about it, Bennett; how did we get back from Sweden? Do you remember the plan we made?"

"You guys went to Sweden? When was that? I don't remember you going anywhere, Bennett," Owen said.

"But I can guess how you got home; you flew...or took a boat, right?"

"Not exactly," Bennett reluctantly told his friend. "Should I tell him, or do you want to have the honor?" he asked his sister.

"You go right ahead, little brother."

"Okay, Owen...let's back up a bit," Bennett suggested. "Earlier today, we talked about how when Susie wore her shoes to bed and we talked about a famous person or place we wanted to visit, the next thing we knew, we would be there. Well, you know, we think that last night, when you were sleeping over and she was helping us with our research about world hunger by once again reading to us from the biography about Audrey Hepburn, we think the shoes caused us to travel back in time to where we now find ourselves, in Somalia, right?"

Owen seemed to be following the explanation, so Bennett continued. "Well, last year when we were reading about the Nobel Prize, we think we went to Stockholm, Sweden! Not only do we remember going to the award banquet, but we are positive we actually got to meet Madame Curie! Owen, we talked with her, even went to her room in the Grand Hotel. It was awesome...and all because of Susie's shoes! Not only did they get us there, they also got us home."

"Yes, but the soldier took her shoes away; now we don't have them to help us get back home. If they got us here, they certainly won't be able to get us back to Merion now that someone else is wearing them... unless we can find a way to steal them back. Is that what we are going to do?" Owen asked.

Susie took over the discussion. "No, Owen. That's too risky. Bennett and I were talking and had a thought;

maybe we don't need the shoes to get home. In fact, when we were in Sweden, we figured out that it's when I take the shoes *off* and go to sleep that we end up back in our own beds. I have to take my shoes off for us to make it home."

"We're thinking that since they stole my sister's shoes and she is going to sleep without them on, when we wake up, we will be back in Pennsylvania. At least, that is what we are hoping will happen," Bennett said.

"However, don't think for one minute that we won't try to bring my shoes along with us," Susie added.

Although this made Owen more hopeful, he could not help but notice Susie still seemed upset. "What's the matter, Susie?" he asked. "This is good news, isn't it?"

Susie surprised herself by how emotional she was becoming. "But what if I can't bring my shoes back with us? When I think about that possibility, it just makes me so sad...and angry."

There was a huge lump in her throat, this time not because of the red, dusty air that surrounded her. She was upset at the thought of leaving her granny's shoes in Africa. How would she tell her family? What would they think? Would they even believe her when she told her mother, father, and grandmother where she had left them?

The truth was, she did not know if they would make it home, although she was convinced it was necessary to take off her shoes in order to return to her own room. But now that they no longer belonged to her, she did not know what to expect.

In a flash, another thought crossed her mind; what if the little African girl went to sleep wearing the shoes? Where would she wake up? And what if she took them off at bedtime; would she wake up in Susie's room? One way or another, Susie knew they would soon find out.

She was relieved that her brother and Owen had cuddled up next to Kagiso, buried in a deep pile of hay. The straw appeared to sparkle in the moonlight, giving off its own glow, much like the way Susie's shoes did when she wore them.

Susie could not wait to fall asleep, hoping she would find herself in Merion, Pennsylvania when the sun came up. She was more worried about telling her granny the bad news about her shoes than about whether they would all be able to get home again. And although she had put on a brave face for the boys, she was keenly aware that day might never come.

CHAPTER EIGHT

Oh, to Be Back Home in my Own Bed

There were no birds where they were in Africa. That was one of the things Susie missed most, the familiar sounds of her life back at home. Somalia was filled with the cries of hungry, young babies, the report of guns the soldiers used to scare and control the villagers, and the ever-present groans of the elderly as they tried to keep up with the rebels' commands.

So when Susie thought she heard the melody of the wind chime that was attached to the bird feeder outside her window, she wanted to see if the finches were back. But she would have to open her eyes to do so...and she was afraid.

When she took a deep breath to prepare herself for whatever would happen, Susie was surprised by how easy it was to breathe; no hint of the hot air that was filled with red dust from the African desert floor. And now she could hear the birds chirping in the tree next to her side of the house.

As she slowly opened her eyes, she was greeted by her pink-and-white-striped wallpaper and twin beds. There was no pile of hay anywhere to be seen. She was home!

When she sat up in her bed, the next thing Susie did was look down at her feet. They were so dirty... and they were very sore. It was then she remembered her birthday shoes had been taken from her...and she began to weep. It had been a long time since Susie felt so helpless...maybe not since that spring day when her brother had been run over by a car, right in front of their house.

How would she ever get the courage to tell her granny what had happened? While Susie knew she had been right to hope that going to sleep without her precious shoes on might bring her and the boys home, she still felt loss and sadness.

At the same time, compared to the plight of the people they had left behind in Somalia, Susie was ashamed that she was so upset about a birthday present; she knew the children and villagers were still hungry and would be hungry for days to come, unless the supplies the United Nations had brought to Bidoa were dispersed.

"Enough of this self-pity!" Susie said out loud. Suddenly she realized she had to find her brother. What would she do if he wasn't in his room? And she would have to check on Owen too. While her family seemed to know there might be some magic associated with her granny's present, how would she explain their visit to Africa to Limpho and Baruti Kane, if their son was nowhere to be found?

She swung her legs over the side of her bed to make her way into Bennett's room. As her feet touched the floor, she almost tripped...over her shoes! Not only had she made it back home, but so had her granny's most wondrous gift.

As quickly as she could, Susie put on her red shoes and rushed across the hall to see if her brother and Owen were okay. Now she had little doubt about their safe return and could not wait to tell them the good news.

Susie gently knocked on her brother's door, so as not to scare him, and made her way across his bedroom. Because the shades were still drawn, the room was dark, but Susie could see that Bennett and Owen were sound asleep in his bed.

It wasn't the sound of his sister's footsteps but the red glow that filled his room that caused Bennett to stir and turn over. He was happy and relieved to see his sister, but the first words out of his mouth were, "You got them back...your shoes! And they haven't lost their glow."

"Hey, you guys; I'm trying to sleep over here."

Of course Owen was in her brother's room. She had been reading to the boys from her birthday book the night their journey began.

"Owen, wake up," Bennett told his friend. "We're home! We made it! We're out of Africa, my friend."

"That was one of my favorite movies," Karen Gardner said, as she entered her son's bedroom after hearing Susie knock on his door. "And you're wearing your shoes, my darling. I hope you didn't fall asleep with them on."

"Don't even go there," Owen said. "Let's just say I am especially happy to see you, Mrs. Gardner...and not because I can tell you made that famous cake of yours."

"You're right, Owen. I just took it out of the oven. My mother is coming for a visit and I always make it for her arrival."

"Oh, wow!" Susie said, as she quickly turned and ran out of her brother's bedroom. "I have to call Granny Ella. Something has happened that can't wait for tomorrow. See ya," she called back to her family as she rushed out of the room.

CHAPTER NINE

Help from Granny Ella

"It's so good to hear from you, darling!" Susie's grandmother told her. "Did you know I am coming for a visit Monday afternoon, or were your parents keeping it as a surprise? Oh, I may have ruined things."

"Oh, no, Granny. Mom just mentioned your visit and everyone is so excited. Actually, we knew before she told us...she didn't have to say a word. As soon as we woke up, we could smell the chewy, gooey, dark chocolate fudge cake she made...just for you, Granny Ella."

"So what is it that can't wait until tomorrow, my dear? You have made me curious. Is everything alright?"

Even though things had worked out in a kind of surprising way, the trip to Africa was still fresh in Susie's mind and still the source of much sadness in her heart. So much starvation, so many tears...and now Susie was worried about what Kagiso would think when she woke up and found them gone.

There was no way to get a message to Kagiso, no way to let her know they were okay. Bennett and Owen were positive they had traveled back to 1992, as that was the year when Audrey Hepburn came to Somalia... seventeen years ago. Who knew if the villagers were still alive? And Susie wondered what happened when the soldier saw that his daughter's new shoes were missing? Surely his little girl would be upset. Was there a chance he would suspect Kagiso had something to do with the child's disappointment? And, if so, could Kagiso's life be in even more danger? Would her brother be able to protect her and the other villagers if the rebel tried to take his frustration out on them?

Before she called her Granny Ella, Susie went on her computer to research Somalia on her own. She was especially interested in finding out whether the name 'Kagiso' had any special meaning. When she found out it meant 'peace', she was relieved. She remembered the moments when the older woman had intervened, trying to help her people stay calm and not letting the rebels treat them any more unkindly. Yes, that was a fitting name for her friend.

The first question Susie asked her granny took Ella by surprise. "Granny...what would happen if someone took the magical shoes? Or what if I lost them...left them somewhere? Don't worry; I have them on right now. But I was wondering just the same."

"Well, dear, that is an interesting question...and I have the answer you are looking for...and probably were hoping for too. I must have been about twelve years old when we went to a family reunion in Pittsburgh. We were so excited to get to visit with our relatives. This was around 1926. Our Granny Didi paid for everything, including for my parents, brothers and sisters, and me to stay in a wonderful, fancy hotel. All five of us girls shared two queen-sized beds. Oh, it was so much fun! We stayed up all night and took turns putting makeup on each other and polishing our nails. We got very little sleep and were tired our first day there."

"Did you wear your shoes on that trip, Granny?"

"Yes, my dear. And that was a big mistake. The whole family knew about the shoes and there was no good reason to take them with me. But I just loved them so much; I knew we would see my Granny Didi who gave them to me, and I guess I just wanted her to see how much I adored them."

"Well, the day after we arrived, the whole family went to visit the Phipps Conservatory and Botanical Gardens. That may have been the moment I decided I would become a master gardener myself. What a magnificent place that was. It was built in 1893, so it had been opened for about thirty-three years when I saw it for the first time. I will have to take you there someday, my dear."

"Anyway, my mother would not let me wear my shoes to the garden, so we left them by the side of my bed in the hotel. By the end of the day, we were so exhausted, especially those of us who had been up all night. Before we went to my grandmother's house for dinner, we went back to the hotel to freshen up. Of course, I was going to wear my red shoes that she had given me four years earlier, but when I looked by the side of my bed, they were not where I had left them."

"You can imagine just how upset I was. At first I thought one of my brothers had hidden them as a joke; they were always doing things like that to my sisters and me. But when my father questioned them, they swore they had no idea where they could be. Believe me, my brothers would not have lied to my father, so we assumed someone in the hotel had stolen them."

"How terrible, Granny. What did you do?"

"There was nothing to do but hope they would somehow show up. That night, I went to bed crying... I was inconsolable. I did not tell my grandmother because I did not want to upset her after all the trouble she went to bringing the family together for such a lovely dinner and reunion."

"But the next morning, a miracle had happened. When I got up to get dressed, there were my shoes, right where I had left them. They came back to me. Oh, I was over-the-moon with happiness!"

"Did you ever find out what had happened to them, Granny?" Susie asked.

"No, dear. But when I saw my grandmother the next day, I told her all about what had happened. And here is what she told me. She said, 'I have given those shoes to you, Ella, my first granddaughter, and they belong to you and only you, until the time you give them to your own first granddaughter. Someone may take them, someone may try to destroy them, but they will always come back to their rightful owner. You cannot give them away to a friend or even donate them to a charity. You can only give them to your first granddaughter...and she can only give them to her own first granddaughter."

Susie noticed her grandmother seemed sure and confident about what she was saying. There was a tone to her voice that the young granddaughter had never heard before. Susie always knew these shoes were an important and treasured family heirloom, but to Granny Ella, they seemed to be even more than that.

As Susie took a moment to reflect, two things came to mind. First, when her grandmother said, "You can only give them to your first granddaughter," Susie realized the implication of those words. Of course, there had been times when she thought about being a mother. She had an impressive doll collection and, when she was younger, she would pretend the dolls were her children. And she loved her brother with all her heart; as she helped him through difficult times, she had imagined this was what it would be like to have a child of her own. However, until Granny Ella had just mentioned the day when she would have her own granddaughter, Susie had never considered what the distant future could look like.

Secondly, it occurred to her that these shoes were much more than a gift or family tradition; they carried with them a much larger responsibility. She thought back to the little girl in Somalia whose father had taken them. To his young daughter, they were a beautiful pair of shoes…maybe even the first pair of shoes she had ever had. How sad she must have been to wake up and find them gone. She may have been even more upset than Susie was when they went missing. And if Kagiso were blamed for their disappearance, she could be in serious danger. So the shoes were capable of causing fear and sadness, even death, if their owner was not mindful of their powers.

"I am guessing something happened to the shoes, my dear, for you to be asking me these questions," Granny Ella said.

"Oh, Granny, you know me so well. When you come to visit tomorrow, I will tell you all about my latest experience with your birthday gift. For now, just know everything is fine...great even. Yes, there is a lot for us to talk about tomorrow night."

"And we will have our favorite bedtime snack. Ummmm...I can already taste it," Granny Ella said.

"Me too, Ella Bella. This is the best news I could have gotten, that you are coming to visit, other than finding out my shoes were back." As soon as Susie heard herself, she realized she had spilled the beans.

"There is so much more to your special birthday present. Yes, we will have a lot to talk about over the next few days. For now, sleep tight...and don't let the bed bugs bite," her grandmother said.

"Oh, Granny...you should have seen the size of the bugs I saw in Africa! They were ugly, disgusting, and so horrible. And some people even *eat* them! No, we won't spend our time talking about them," Susie said, not realizing she had told her granny much more than she had intended to.

CHAPTER TEN

Back to Reality

Owen was exhausted when he got home from the Gardners', early Sunday evening. When they were finished with dinner, his father asked him, "I know you are working hard on your hunger project, my son, but are you able to keep up with the rest of your school work? Tomorrow is a school day and we are here if you need our help with anything."

Suddenly, Owen realized the rough draft of his book report was due tomorrow and he hadn't even started it. "I may take you up on that," he told his parents as he left the table and went up to his room.

Owen had enjoyed reading Norman Maclean's *A River Runs Through It*. Actually, it would be more accurate to say he enjoyed listening to the story; although he had carefully followed along in the book he had borrowed from the library, Owen had used his TTS software, to make sure he understood and remembered his favorite parts.

The story was based on Mr. Maclean's own experiences growing up in Montana, so Owen knew that meant it was autobiographical. But he was surprised when he found out the book was referred to as a 'novella', or a short novel. He had never heard that word before, at least not that he remembered. However, given his learning problems, it turned out to be a good thing that the book was shorter, rather than longer.

His teacher had suggested that he read the classic tale of the two brothers who grew up in Missoula, Montana. As he read along with the help of his computer, he discovered the boys' father was a Presbyterian minister and the two sons were as different as two boys could be. Norman, the author, was quite studious and became a teacher, while his brother Paul was more rebellious and became a journalist.

When they were growing up, the brothers spent their mornings in school and studying religion; however, in the afternoons, they went fly fishing in the nearby Blackfoot River. It was during their times by the water that the boys were best able to relate to each other. It seemed to Owen that even though they spent more hours during their week in religious studies with their father, their experiences fly fishing in the river were more spiritual.

Owen related to this story, even more so since his travels to Somalia. His new-found feelings for his homeland had given him the same sense of love for what mattered most...family, friends, community, and helping others, that filled his heart as he read Norman Maclean's first book. But now, Owen had to get to work.

As he thought about the paper he was supposed to write, and on what aspect of the story he wanted to focus, he realized that, in the end, the book was a tribute to brotherhood. Although he did not have a brother, he could see similarities to what Mr. Maclean had written about in the ups and downs of his relationship with his younger sister. Maybe he would write a summary of the story and then compare his life with his sister to that of the brothers.

With that in mind, Owen drew a story web to help him organize his thoughts. After dividing the middle into five sections, with a few notes about the things he needed to include in the story summary, he decided there were actually four parts of the story that reminded him of life with Katie. Owen knew he needed an introductory sentence, at least three detail sentences, and a concluding sentence for each paragraph he wrote, one for each comparison he would make.

When he had finished his organizer and realized he was looking at a ten-paragraph paper, Owen became overwhelmed. Once again, he had waited until the last minute to get going on an assignment. Even with the help of his computer, any written project was a daunting task for him. The more he thought about what needed to get done, the more worried he became. Just as his mother had told him, his fear of not finishing was preventing him from even starting the written report. And, with the added distraction of the possible student government hunger project, not to mention the trip to Africa...oh, he had almost forgotten about that adventure...he could not imagine how he would get his work done in time.

He knew he could not afford to think about anything but his report. It was getting late. Focus, focus, he reminded himself. Once he got going, it only took him about twenty minutes to finish the book summary portion of his paper.

It was the comparison between his life and that of the Maclean brothers that was more challenging. As he looked at his story web, he saw he had already identified the four comparisons he wanted to make. But the words just would not come to him.

Although the house was quiet, Owen thought he heard someone outside his bedroom door. It could not be his sister as it was already past her bedtime. In the next moment, he heard a gentle knock that he recognized as his mother's.

"Come in, Mom," Owen said. "This is perfect timing; I'm stuck and need some help."

"That's what I am here for, my son. It looks like you have made some good progress," his mother said in her encouraging way. "Can I see what you have already completed? I have read the book you are writing about and may be able to be of assistance."

Owen thanked his mom for her offer. He immediately felt more confident, just knowing she was there. He had noticed that, most of the time when he worked with his tutor, he did not need her to do anything at all besides sit at his side as he worked. He was starting to believe his school was right and that his problems were mostly related to his inability to stay focused, especially when his fear of failure prevented him from taking that first big step of beginning a project.

"Owen, this is wonderful!" his mother remarked. "As far as I can remember, you have done a beautiful job capturing the essence of the story...and you accomplished this without giving away too many of the details, so your friends won't feel like they know what happens without having to read the book. In fact, I'll bet they will all *want* to read it."

Now came the hard part for Limpho...how to show her son the things he would have to fix, even with a computer that continuously checked for spelling errors. One of Owen's biggest problems was substituting a real word for another that sounded similar, and the spell-checker feature did not find and correct these mistakes. She knew this was related to what Dr. Roberts had called her son's "auditory processing disorder".

Limpho decided they should finish the report before making any corrections. She was concerned her son might become disheartened if he was made aware of the changes that were still needed.

Over the next hour, they finished the comparisons Owen wanted to make between his life with Katie and Norman Maclean's life with his brother Paul. Limpho knew it was important for Owen to feel he could edit his work himself. Rather than make the corrections herself, she took a blue pen and circled the words she wanted him to reconsider, just as she has seen his tutor do. And, even though it took another thirty minutes for him to make all the changes, in the end, he was proud of the report he had written.

It was now way past Owen's bedtime and he could not wait to get into his own, comfy bed; it seemed like it had been days since he had done so. He remembered lying on the hard, red earth in Somalia, wishing he were right where he was now, ready to sleep in his own room, in his own house, away from the dust and sadness that surrounded the people of his native homeland.

After he washed and his mother tucked him in, Owen was about to drift off to slumber when he heard his mother and father whispering in the hall, right outside his door. Limpho thought her son was sound asleep when she left his room, or she never would have spoken with Baruti at that moment.

"It just breaks my heart to see him struggle so much," Limpho said. "Dear husband, you will have to come and see this school. The Academy In Manayunk is such a glorious place; the children are so beautiful and so smart, just like our son. You would never know they had any learning problems. And the teachers are brilliant. In fact, the school not only trains the teachers who work there, but offers courses to teachers who come from all over the country, even from other countries, to learn their methods. They call the school 'AIM'...and part of their motto is to help the students 'aim for the stars'!"

"Each student has a computer...and they all use the same software programs our son has...and so many more. And Baruti, there are no more than eight children in a class, so the teachers are able to give each student the attention that is needed. Our son would not have to work with a tutor when he got home from school; he would be able to have more time to do the things he wants to do in the afternoons, rather than have more school after school."

By now, Owen was wide awake, sitting up in bed, listening to his parents. Even though he had to admit this school sounded like a special place, a school that might even be able to help him, the thought of leaving Merion Elementary was impossible to imagine.

"My darling wife...this does sound like something we should look into and consider doing for our son. I will go with you and see for myself. However, if we agree this could be a good place for Owen, it will be our son who needs to visit this AIM school. We will have to learn more about it and then see if Owen will consent to consider it. He is such a smart boy and has such a kind heart. He is also motivated to make something of his life, and I feel we can trust him to make the right decision for his future. So, call the school and let's go in together."

"I think this is wise," Limpho said, "although it is not something I think we should consider doing at this point in the school year; maybe fifth grade would be a good time for the change. But you are right; we must trust our son to make the decision. I will call them first thing tomorrow."

Owen could deal with this. It sounded like his parents would let him make the decision. All he had to do was say, "No way!" and it would be the end of the discussion. The last thing he remembered before he drifted off to sleep was wondering if there might be a chance he could actually like the Academy In Manayunk.

CHAPTER ELEVEN

Is a New Star About to Be Born?

"Would Susie Gardner please report to the office?… Susie Gardner, please come to the office now," the loud speaker blared.

Although Susie was a 'cup-is-half-full' person, most of the students at Merion Elementary School thought that being called to the office was not usually a good thing. The announcement took her by surprise and was somewhat alarming; it was almost two in the afternoon and her class was in the middle of a history lesson. She could not help but wonder if something was wrong.

There was a collective "Ooooooh" before Mrs. Magen, the fifth-grade teacher, quieted everyone down. "Now, boys and girls, there is no need to make a fuss. Susie, why don't you walk over to the office and find out what's going on?"

Just as Susie stood up to go, her good friend Madeline Barnett asked, "Can I go with her? Pleeeeease? Susie shouldn't be alone, just in case something terrible has happened."

But before Mrs. Magen could respond, another announcement was made. "Madeline Barnett...would you come to the office with Miss Gardner?...Madeline Barnett, please come to the office."

Now the class was in a real tizzy. Their teacher turned the overhead light switch on and off two times; her students knew that meant they needed to settle down. When they were calm enough to listen she said, "Boys and girls...being called to the office is not necessarily a bad thing. Remember last week when Dylan was called in to meet with Mr. Edney? Son, please tell the class what that was all about."

The young boy stood up and said, "My father came back from Iraq a month early and he showed up at school to surprise me. Hey, maybe there is a special surprise waiting for both of you."

"Exactly what I was talking about! Susie, you and Madeline make your way to the office and I will meet with you after school to bring you up to speed on the discussion we are finishing up. Don't worry; this will be fine."

As Susie and her friend walked down the hall on their way to the office, they giggled and guessed what might be in store for them.

"Maybe we won a trip to Disneyland," Madeline said. "Or maybe Disney World...that's closer."

"Oh, I hope not. I think I've done enough traveling lately," Susie said, without stopping to think before she spoke. No one besides her brother and Owen Kane knew about her magical adventures...well, maybe her granny did too. And even though she and Madeline had a wonderful friendship, Susie knew, in some ways, the power of her shoes could be a burden. She had to be careful about what she said. And sometimes she felt like she should lie, in order to keep the secret of her granny's gift. So far, that hadn't been necessary; by quickly changing the subject when she or Bennett slipped up, they were able to avert disaster. And now, she would have to put that approach to the test.

"What traveling?" her friend asked. "I didn't know you had been anywhere. Did your family take a trip you didn't tell me about?"

"Oh, not a real trip; I've been helping one of my brother's friends with a project he is doing on world hunger. We have been reading so much about Somalia and other starving countries, it just *feels* like I've been visiting them, the information is so vivid and upsetting."

Luckily, before Madeline could ask Susie any more questions, they arrived at the office. When Principal Edney pointed in their direction, it appeared to the girls that he had been waiting for them. There was a woman standing with him and, as he turned to say something to her, the girls sensed her presence was related to their office visit.

As they walked into the office, Mr. Edney greeted them and said, "Miss Gardner...Miss Barnett, I would like you to meet Kay Hodges; she is visiting us from Lower Merion High School. Besides teaching English Literature, she is also the school's drama coach and works with the students who are members of the *International Thespian Society*."

"I've been looking forward to meeting both of you girls," the tall and beautiful drama teacher said, as she shook hands with the two fifth graders. "Mr. Edney has told me so much about you. So now I suppose you are wondering why we asked you to meet with us."

Madeline spoke right up and said, "We were hoping maybe we had won a trip to Disney World, or something like that."

"Well, I can see you have quite an imagination, young lady...and that is part of why I wanted to meet the two of you. Maybe not a trip to Florida, but, in a way, you both might have the chance to visit Austria... our school's version of Austria, that is."

The two friends looked at each other, burst into giggles, and then hugged each other. Ms. Hodges knew she had to quickly clarify her words before they were disappointed.

"What I am talking about is the fact that our chapter of the *International Thespian Society*, troupe 801, is producing the play, *The Sound of Music*. We named our student group the *Players* and we are one of the few student-run theater programs in the state of Pennsylvania."

"The play we will perform takes place in the mountains of Austria during World War II, and is the story of a remarkable family and their governess. There are six children in the Von Trappe household and we need two young girls to play the part of two of the daughters," Ms. Hodges told Susie and Madeline.

As she continued, the girls began to understand what was involved. "The play is a musical and all the characters have to be able to sing and dance. Mr. Edney tells me you are both very talented, sing in the school chorus, and are not afraid to stand up in front of an audience. Is that true?" she asked.

Susie said, "If you are asking if we are shy, well, not at all; Madeline is a member of the student government and is always getting our classmates to volunteer for this activity or that. She is a real leader. As for me, well, I love an audience!"

"That's the truth," Madeline added. "Susie also has quite an imagination too; when she studies things that happened in history, she sometimes thinks she was alive during that time. She is very dramatic, I would say."

"Well, I'm glad to hear this, ladies. You should know, we will be rehearsing most days after school and sometimes over the weekend. As the parts we want you to play do not appear in every scene, there will be days when you do not need to be at a rehearsal. But it will be a lot of work, besides your school work. Mr. Edney assured me you are both good students; do you think this could interfere with your classes? Are you up for this?"

In unison, the girls said, "Absolutely not!...And yes!"

Now it was their principal's turn to speak. "I thought the two of you would be perfect for this opportunity. Ms. Hodges has the permission forms you will need to have your parents sign. And I will go and speak with your teachers to make sure they are on board. To help make this possible, I'll arrange for the school bus to drop you off at the high school during the week. But your parents will have to get you to the rehearsals on the weekends."

"When is the play going to be performed?" Susie asked.

"A good question," Ms. Hodges responded. "The play is the weekend after Halloween. So we have about six weeks to get ready for opening night. First, we will need to teach you the songs your characters sing and the dances the children in the family perform. Next, we will block the staging, which means show you where you stand and move during your scenes. Then you will have to memorize your lines; you can work together on that, but just know you do not have a lot of dialogue to learn...mostly singing and dancing."

"This sounds like so much fun," Susie said.

"Alright then," Mr. Edney said, as he brought the discussion to a close. "Please go back to your class and I will meet with your teachers. I guess there is just one other thing to say...'break-a-leg'!"

"What?" said Madeline.

Susie took her friend's hand and pulled her along, out of the office, as they saw both the drama teacher and principal start to laugh. "Haven't you ever heard that before?" Susie asked Madeline.

"Well, no; why would he say that to us? If we break a leg we won't be able to dance in the show!"

"What am I going to do with you, Madeline? That's a theater expression...it means 'good luck'."

Her friend looked at her and said, "I don't know, Susie. Am I cut out for this?"

"We will both be stars; have no fear."

CHAPTER TWELVE

Rhyming is Not Such a Bad Thing

When school was over, Susie looked all over for Bennett; she wanted to tell him her good news. First, she went to his classroom and he was not there. Then she asked some of his friends if they knew where he was, and no one had seen him since the final bell had rung.

It was Carl Tracker who told her he had overheard Bennett and Owen talking about doing some work at the Kanes' house. The two boys had been spending a lot of time together, especially since their adventure in Africa...at least Susie thought they had all visited Somalia; either that or she, her brother, and their friend Owen had all had the same exact dream on the exact same night.

Susie had an idea about what the boys might be working on, so she put the permission form for the high school play in her schoolbag and made her way home. She felt certain her mother would be almost as excited as she was about the upcoming performance and couldn't wait to tell her. Susie had no doubt her parents would want her to participate.

Back at the Kane house, the boys had just walked into Owen's kitchen and found a snack and note from his mother. "Mom left us all these brownies, Bennett, and this note says she is going to be late getting home from work. She must have guessed you'd be coming over as she also says to tell you she talked to your mom and it's okay for you to sleep over tonight."

"Great!" Bennett said, as he picked up a brownie and began to eat. "Mmmmm…boy…these are soooo delicious…almost as good as my granny's cake, don't you think?"

"With work and all, my mom doesn't often have the time to do much baking. I'll bet she got these from 'The Chocolate Kitchen'." As Owen took a bite, he said, "You're right on two counts; one, they are yummy, and two, that chewy, gooey, dark chocolate fudge cake your mother makes is still the best!"

The boys inhaled their snacks and made their way up to Owen's bedroom. "Come see what I found out about hunger in America," Owen told his friend, as they sat side-by-side at his computer.

"You're so lucky to have your own laptop. I have to use the one in our family room or borrow my sister's," Bennett said.

"Well, I'm not so lucky to have all these learning problems; it was the school that told my parents I needed to do my work on the computer. Have you ever tried to read my handwriting?"

"Now that you mention it, when we were working at the library on our science project last year, I did notice you have a…what should I call it?…unusual way of writing things down. I knew you knew what you were writing, but if I had to guess…"

"Say no more," Owen said and laughed at his friend's way of trying to be kind. "Let's just agree that if I want to get the kind of grades I should be getting, I have to type all my work. Did you notice that I often leave the room when we are having tests? Well, that's because I take them in the Learning Center. That way I can type my answers and, if there is a lot of reading on the exam, the computer can read me the questions. Look here…there's a program I use so that when I come to a word I don't know, I can highlight it and press a button…and it will say the word and tell me what it means. How cool is that?"

"Wow, that is *really* cool! So where is all this stuff about hunger? Is it as bad in our country as it is in Africa?"

"It's different. Think about all the money we now have in America and the fact that we are a nation that has the knowledge and benefits of the wealthy countries from where our founding fathers came. Now think about how little the villagers in Africa have; they never had the advantages we do. So, for me, starvation here in America may be even more outrageous."

"Don't get me wrong; what is happening in Somalia and all over Africa is more than horrible. And I *will* find a way to do something about that too. But my resource teacher has told me that sometimes we have to "go slow to grow" and, for now, I think we should focus on the people in our own community and the towns nearby. What do you think, Bennett?"

"I agree with you, oh brilliant fourth-grade student government rep."

"So I was thinking. We need a slogan. Now, don't laugh; remember when we picketed the country club and you gave us that line we used for our posters? I know, I know; you don't speak in rhyme any more. But rhymes are catchy; people remember them."

Owen continued, "Do you also remember when we raised all that money for the United Nations on Halloween of last year? Well, I was thinking about a food drive we had at our church for the local Food Cupboard two weeks ago. Each person in the congregation who came to the service that Sunday had to bring along a bag of groceries...not food that would spoil, but things that would keep on the shelves... things in cans and sealed in boxes. You can't believe how much food we collected."

"Are you thinking of trick-or-treating for food instead of money or candy?" Bennett asked.

"Maybe," Owen replied. "What do you think about calling our project 'Trick-or-Treating So Kids Are Eating'? Here, let's *Google* it and see what comes up."

While they did not find anyone using that exact phrase, something amazing stared back at them from Owen's computer screen. "Oh, wow!" Bennett said. "Look at the first entry. It looks like there already may be someone doing what we want to do, but they call it, *Trick or Treat so Kids Can Eat...TOTS-EAT* for short."

"Let's see what that's all about," Owen suggested.

As the boys clicked on the slogan, they could not believe what they were reading. Yes, there was a program that focused on hunger in America and it involved students of all ages collecting food for the needy.

"It looks like kids have been doing this since 2003! Why didn't we hear about this?" Bennett wondered.

"Well, the good news is we know about it now. It seems like we can choose whatever food banks we want and give them the donations we collect. Let's see if it tells us how to organize all this. I wonder how we would get the word out about the project," Owen said.

"Look at this...boy, they really know what they are doing. There is no way we could ever do as good a job as they have done. And why should we even try? It's all right here. Let's see how we get started," Bennett suggested.

"It says we have to register as a troupe. What's a 'troupe'?" Owen asked.

"It looks like this program is sponsored by the *International Thespian Society*; let's read some more," Bennett said.

As the boys got deeper and deeper into their research, Bennett realized he would have to do most of the reading. He could tell his friend struggled with some of the words. "From what this says, I think these 'thespians' are part of a theater organization...look at this; they spell 'theater' with an *re* instead of *er*."

"Just what I need," Owen said. "A new way to spell a word I thought I already knew!"

Bennett just kept moving through the information to keep his friend from focusing on his problems. "This is cool, Owen. A 'troupe' is a group of actors, and the *International Thespian Society* sponsors these troupes in both middle and high schools. It's an 'honorary organization'...I think that means it's a privilege to join."

"But we're an elementary school; can we still do this with *TOTS-EAT*?" Owen asked.

"We might have to join forces with one of the local high schools," Bennett replied. "Let's see if either Harriton or Lower Merion is a member of the *ITS*."

Bennett went to *ask.com* and found out that although Harriton had a drama club, they were not *ITS* members. "But Lower Merion High School is! They are troupe 801 and call themselves the *Players.* Owen, this could end up being pretty amazing, don't you think? I'll bet our student government would love to do a project with the high school."

CHAPTER THIRTEEN

I Can Already Taste the Cake!

Susie had so many exciting things going on at the same time, she did not know what to tell her grandmother about first. As she made her way home from school, she decided she would start with her role in the high school play. She thought her mother would also be there to greet her and, until she talked to her granny about her apparent trip to Somalia, she did not want to alarm her mother unnecessarily, in case it was all just a dream.

Granny Ella was waiting by the kitchen door, just as her young granddaughter knew she would be. Susie rushed in and gave her a big, long hug. When she saw her mother smiling back at the two of them from the sink, Susie knew she deserved some loving attention too, and went over to kiss her warm cheek.

Susie noticed the chewy, gooey, dark chocolate fudge cake sitting in the middle of the kitchen table, along with three place settings. When Karen Gardner saw her daughter looking in that direction, she said, "Okay, lovely ladies. Let's dig in!"

It was so wonderful having Granny Ella there. Coming home from school and seeing her standing in their kitchen reminded Susie of the year her dad worked in Italy and Granny Ella stayed with them to help with the extra load her mother had to carry.

"Mom," Karen began, "we have some exciting good news to tell you about. Susie is going to be one of the stars of the high school's play! Tell your granny all about it, my darling."

At first, Susie was surprised her mother already knew about her role in the production. But then she figured Mr. Edney called to get her approval, before Susie was even called to the office.

The look on her mother's face made Susie so proud. It was not often she had her mother to herself when she came home from school; Bennett was usually right behind her. This alone-time felt wonderful, especially sharing it with Granny Ella. Just the three of them.

"Oh, it's so exciting. I have to learn five different songs and all the dancing that goes with them. And, of course, there are some lines I have to memorize too. We have our first rehearsal tomorrow and I can't wait. You'll still be here when I get back, won't you, Granny? By then I'll have my script and maybe you could help me and my friend Madeline learn our parts."

"My darling, I cannot think of anything I would rather do, besides hear more about this business with Africa," her grandmother said.

Susie was shocked her granny would mention their phone conversation in front of her mother. It was never quite clear to Susie just how much her mother knew about the red birthday shoes, but common sense suggested she knew more than she let on. After all, the shoes had belonged to Granny Ella for all those years before she gave them to Susie. Karen had grown up seeing those shoes on her mother's feet.

"You know, Susie," her mother began, "there were times growing up when my mother seemed distant… even confused. You can imagine how close your granny and I were…and still are. But as a young child, it sometimes seemed like she was off somewhere, figuratively speaking…off in her own world. It worried me, even scared me from time to time."

"So you can see how I felt," Granny Ella added. "There *were* times when it seemed I really *was* off somewhere, my darlings…and it was so confusing to me as well."

"At first, I only had those feelings when I wore the shoes my grandmother Didi had given to me, so I stopped wearing them for a time. But they were so special that I put them on again at a later date, only to have the same sensation of having gone some place."

"I know what you mean, Granny," Susie replied. "Mom, do you think wearing the shoes can make time-travel possible?"

"Your grandmother and I have talked a lot about this over the years and we still do not know the truth about what these shoes can and cannot do. But, in the end, whether they do possess magical powers or just make it possible for you to be your most imaginative self and dream impossible dreams, is not the issue. What is most important is that they are a special family tradition that has kept us all guessing for many years."

Susie knew her mother was partially right, but perhaps did not realize all the implications of the shoes.

Susie had seen first-hand how the shoes could make it possible for the wearer to witness history in the making...at least she thought they could.

As the three of them talked some more, Susie knew this would not be the last discussion she would have about the special birthday gift her granny had given her. One thing she knew for sure; she could confide in her mother as her dreams or time-travel adventures presented themselves. And that was a big relief.

CHAPTER FOURTEEN

More Research

Bennett kept reading and was amazed by what he found. "Owen, listen to this; the *ITS* was founded in 1929, more than thirty years ago...and, since then, more than two million students have joined. There are almost four thousand schools around the world that are a part of this organization. This is a big deal! And it looks like the *ITS* is a division of the *Educational Theatre Association*. We need to find out more about them."

"This is a timeline of the *ETA*; read this part," Owen asked.

"Okay, here we go. It looks like a man by the name of Dr. Earl Blank, a teacher at Natrona County High School in Casper, Wyoming, suggested the idea of an organization for high school theater students to his friend Dr. Paul Opp."

"Where did he live?" Owen asked.

"Dr. Opp was a college professor at Fairmont State College in West Virginia. He began with a series of meetings that included his secretary, Ernest Bavely, and Harry Leeper, a teacher from East Fairmont High School. Together, the three built on this idea of a theater organization for high school students. Mr. Blank's students back in Wyoming were given the first charter to what was then known as *The National Thespians*. Oh, boy. By the end of the next school year, there were seventy-one chartered troupes of *Thespians*."

"What is a 'charter'?" Owen asked Bennett. "Wait, I'll let my TTS program tell us."

Now it was Bennett's turn to ask a question. "What is a 'TTS' program?"

"It's the software I got from school that can turn writing, or 'text', into speech," Owen told his friend.

As Owen highlighted the word 'charter', the boys learned that a charter is like a 'constitution'. It gives people the right to join an organization and tells them the things they can and cannot do while they are members. The boys found out that as more and more high schools formed troupes, the name was changed to *The National Thespian Society*.

After its twenty-fifth anniversary, the name the theater honorary currently goes by, *The International Thespian Society*, was announced. By that time, there were chapters in forty-eight states and several territories of the United States, as well as in other countries, such as Canada and Japan.

It was not long before they began a *Junior Thespians* organization to reach out to middle schoolers, and its most recent role was helping to launch a *Senior Theatre League of America*...an independent organization for older actors and theater supporters with whom the *ETA* shares its successes and experiences.

"Owen, it says here the *Educational Theatre Association* is the professional organization for all teachers who are involved in teaching students about the theater. The *ETA* publishes a monthly magazine for their students and teachers called *Dramatics*, and one just for teachers called *Teaching Theatre*."

"Let's go back to the page that told us what we have to do to get started," Owen suggested.

The boys had already figured out the high school troupe would have to register their *TOTS-EAT* project. There was even a contest to find out which groups around the world had the most successful events. But to be eligible to win one of the prizes, the registration form had to be received by October fifteenth. This meant the student government would have to quickly approve the project request and the boys would have to meet with the *Players* at Lower Merion.

They could see that *ITS* provided the *TOTS-EAT* participants with many materials to support their projects. There were announcement cards to be put in all the neighbors' mailboxes to let them know what would be happening on Halloween and how to organize their donations. There were *TOTS-EAT* buttons for the children to wear when they went trick-or-treating, so the homeowners would know who they were. There were also sample press releases so the local newspapers could promote the projects, as well as thank-you-for-donating cards to give to their generous neighbors once the collection was over.

"Owen, we can do this, but we have to get right on it. We have no time to waste. Let's keep reading and getting our facts in order. After school tomorrow, we'll go to my house and talk to Susie about this. I'll bet she will want to call her friend Madeline and get her opinion," Bennett said.

"I know who she is; Madeline is a member of the student government with me," Owen added. "It would be a good idea to show up at school with at least one other SG member on our side."

CHAPTER FIFTEEN

A Team Approach

With so many ideas floating around in their heads, it was not surprising the boys couldn't wait till the end of Tuesday's school day to go back to Bennett's house and show his sister what they had learned. Although they had already accomplished a lot, the clock was ticking and there was much more Owen and Bennett needed to get done before the student government meeting on Friday.

As they entered Bennett's house by the kitchen door, they were a little surprised to find a party-like atmosphere where Susie, her mother and father, and Granny Ella were laughing and eating the famous chewy, gooey, dark chocolate fudge cake. With everything that was going on, Bennett had completely forgotten about his grandmother's arrival.

"What's up, you guys?" Bennett questioned his family as he ran over to hug his grandmother. "This feels like a celebration. Did I miss someone's birthday?"

It was Eric Gardner who told his son and Owen about Susie's and Madeline's exciting news. "The girls have their first rehearsal at Lower Merion High School this evening. The school has a theater group and they are putting on the show, *The Sound of Music.* Their acting troupe needed a few younger students to play some of the parts, and the girls were chosen."

Susie added, "Madeline should be here any moment and then Dad is taking us over to the school. How cool is this?"

While Susie knew her brother would be happy for her, she was not prepared for his over-the-top reaction. Bennett and Owen looked at each other, smiled their toothy grins, and in unison said, "Very, very cool!" as they high-fived each other.

It only took the boys a few minutes to fill Susie, Bennett's parents, and Granny Ella in on what they were hoping to do on Halloween. They spoke so fast, it was hard for Susie to follow all the details. But she recognized the word 'thespians' and *'Players'* from her talk with Ms. Hodges.

"So you want to form a partnership between our school and the high school theater group to collect food for the hungry," Susie summarized.

That was when Owen remembered something else he thought could be important. "You know what? I think we saw an article about a high school in Chicago that was a part of the *International Thespian Society* and did more than just collect food for the hungry on Halloween. I think they sold tickets to their fall play and gave a discount to anyone who showed up to the performance with a bag of canned goods."

"You're right, Owen. Susie, we read that last year the *TOTS-EAT* program collected over 250,000 pounds of canned and packaged food. That's more than 125 tons!" Bennett said.

Now it was Karen Gardner's turn to speak up. "How did the children carry all those heavy bags of food?" she asked. "If we organized the students at our elementary school to do this on Halloween, how would the youngsters deal with the donations?"

Susie had what she thought might be the winning idea. "What if instead of having our parents drive us around trick-or-treating, we had students from the high school take us in their cars? That way, they could join in all the fun and also help carry the heavy bags with us. We could form teams of younger and older kids, based on where the students live. At the end of the night, we could all go back to the high school gym, have a weigh-in, and leave the bags for the Food Cupboard to pick up the next day."

"Tell me again when the play is being performed?" Eric asked his daughter.

"Three times the weekend *after* Halloween! Oh, wow! We just might be able to organize more food drop offs at the shows like you told us they did in Chicago. I'll bet we could bring in enough food to feed our whole town for a week...the needy for months!" Susie exclaimed.

Just then, Madeline arrived for her ride to their first rehearsal. "What's all the excitement about?" she asked.

"I'll tell you in the car," Susie said, and then gave one more suggestion to her brother and Owen before she and Madeline were on their way to Lower Merion. "Boys, I was thinking; since this is our first time meeting and working with the high school actors, maybe we should hold off telling them what we are thinking about. Let us get the lay-of-the-land. Madeline and I will do some snooping and see what we can find out about the *Players*."

Owen agreed. "Actually, Susie; I was thinking we first need to get our own student government on board. Bennett is helping me prepare a presentation for our meeting this coming Friday. Madeline, if you don't have a rehearsal tomorrow, could you come over to my house and help me with this? In fact, now that you are a star, maybe you should be the one to tell the student government reps about our project."

"I still don't totally understand what you all are talking about, Owen, but you know I will support you. It just sounds like you already have a plan in motion and know what you're doing. You should follow through with it and, if there is a presentation needed, I think you're the man to do it. Oh, and we do have rehearsals every day this week...and I'm not a star... yet!"

Karen turned to the girls and said, "We can't wait to see the two of you all dressed in your makeup and costumes. I'm sure you will both 'break-a-leg'!"

"Mom, what a terrible thing to say to them," Bennett replied.

"That's just an expression," Owen said, surprised that he knew and understood something his friend did not. Maybe he was as smart as the school said he was, Owen thought to himself.

CHAPTER SIXTEEN

Is Everyone on Board?

Owen and Bennett spent the next few days preparing for Friday morning's before-school student government meeting. Madeline wanted to be there to help with the important presentation, but she had rehearsals every day after school. The boys kept in touch with her through e-mails; by Thursday evening, Owen was satisfied with the approach he would take and knew there would be at least two votes supporting the hunger project.

When Friday morning arrived, Owen got to school early to set up the posters he would need to convince the rest of the representatives. There were copies of the pre-collection announcement cards with the *TOTS-EAT* logo, the sample press releases for the *Main Line Times* and local TV and radio shows, and thank-you cards to place in the mailboxes of the homes that made donations on Halloween…all to be displayed. It was Bennett's idea to make up sample *TOTS-EAT* buttons for each of the SG reps like the ones the trick-or-treaters would wear to identify themselves as they knocked on their neighbors' doors.

Owen had downloaded the things he thought were most impressive about the *Educational Theatre Association*, the *International Thespian Society*, and the food drive. Then his father showed him how to bind the pages into an impressive-looking booklet; they prepared one for each member of the student government and, yes, 'impressive' was the word to describe the approach Owen was taking.

The actual speech he practiced consisted of excerpts he had highlighted from the booklet he was handing out. The pages he needed to speak from were already tabbed. He was ready to go.

As Bennett was no longer a representative to the student government, he was not allowed to attend the meeting. So he patiently waited outside the door of the auditorium to find out if Owen was successful. He was very proud of the job his friend was doing; now it was a waiting game.

Bennett and Owen had discussed the fact that the speech would have to be short, no more than five minutes, or he could lose his audience. And if he kept his own speech shorter, rather than longer, there would be more time for questions. Bennett knew how passionate Owen was about the project and felt sure he could handle any questions that came his way. In addition, Bennett also knew Owen was much better at explaining things to people when he spoke to them, compared to when he read or wrote a report. So he was quite confident Owen would get the support he needed from the other SG members.

Susie was also anxious to hear what happened at the Friday morning meeting and was waiting with Bennett outside the auditorium. She hoped things went well for the project, but knew this meeting was just the first step they had to take. Susie realized that besides getting the high school to agree to work with them and complete the *TOTS-EAT* registration form, and the SG coming on board, they would also need Mr. Edney to approve the event.

Over the years, their principal had proven himself to be a fair and reasonable school leader. But more than that, Susie knew he was always looking for ways to take the classroom out into the community to fulfill a need. Mr. Edney called this approach 'Service Learning'.

Susie had participated in several of these SL projects, so she was aware they were kind of like 'Community Service', but had an additional component; students had to use skills and topics covered in the classroom in the process of meeting the community need. In other words, it had to be educational.

Considering all the tie-ins with world hunger and the history of the warring rebel clans of Africa, there was no doubt the project would lead to several interesting history lessons. The truth was, Owen had already gathered so much important information on the topic, the teachers would have all the materials they needed. So Susie was looking forward to meeting with their principal, knowing he would likely want them to go ahead with the food drive.

As the opening school bell rang, the student government representatives filed out of the auditorium. At first Susie and Bennett were concerned; their classmates did not look happy. In fact, Bennett thought they looked sad. As their friend Madeline walked by, they heard her respond to one of the other students, "Yes, everything Owen said was true. Millions of children, babies even, have starved to death in Africa.

And there are millions of children in our own country who could be facing the same fate. I have seen the pictures!" It certainly appeared the SG representatives were deeply touched by what Owen had shown them.

Once she passed her friends, Madeline turned and gave them two thumbs-up and a large grin. Owen was the last to leave the auditorium, and he was elated. "They're on board! It was a unanimous vote! And you were right, Susie; our advisor said we now need to meet with Mr. Edney. You know, at one moment, when I was talking about my homeland and they saw that famous picture of Miss Hepburn holding the starving child, many of the representatives had tears in their eyes. And the statistics we got on hunger in America sealed the deal. Our faculty advisor, Mr. Banks, is setting up a meeting with Mr. Edney during our lunch recess. Would the two of you want to come along?"

"Great, Owen," Susie said. "I was hoping you weren't going to say it would be after school, with rehearsals and all."

"Owen, we're so impressed. You did an amazing job pulling all this together," Bennett told him.

"I just had another idea," Susie added. "Assuming we get Mr. Edney's approval at our meeting, would you guys like to come to rehearsal with me and Madeline after school? Maybe this would be the time to bring up the project to the *Players* at Lower Merion. Although we've only had three rehearsals, the students are the best. They are so upbeat about everything…very, pardon the word, 'dramatic' about what they think and believe in. I am positive they will want to help. And Owen, you are just the guy to explain what is involved. So what do you think?"

"Boy…really, Susie? You want me to speak to them?"

"Exactly. There is no one I can think of who could do a better job...and don't forget; Madeline will be there too. Let's sell this to Mr. Edney and move it along."

CHAPTER SEVENTEEN

Playing Ball with the Big Guys

The high school was like a maze. "Don't you get lost?" Bennett asked Susie and Madeline.

"This is like being at college," Owen added, remembering what it was like when they went to the University of Pennsylvania to research their science fair project last fall.

"The first rehearsal, on Tuesday, was crazy; we were roaming around, trying to find the auditorium, and we just kept going round and round. Finally, a cute boy came to our rescue and got us there safe and sound," Madeline told the boys.

"They are taking such good care of us," Susie added. "It kind of feels like we have twenty new brothers and sisters."

As soon as the words came out of her mouth, she saw the smile on Bennett's face disappear. "But none of them are as adorable as you are, Bennett."

"And there are moments when it can be a little annoying; sometimes they act like we're two-year-olds,"

Madeline lamented. "The truth is, everyone was amazed when we learned the words to the first song in fifteen minutes."

"And this afternoon, we are learning a new song and the dance steps that go with it," Susie said. "I hope the *Players* won't mind you watching," she added, just as she saw the director, Ms. Hodges, approach them.

"Hi there, girls!" she greeted them. "And who do we have here?"

Susie said, "This is my brother Bennett and his good friend Owen Kane."

"Owen is the fourth-grade representative to our student government at Merion, Ms. Hodges," Madeline added.

"Welcome to Austria, young men. Do you have any interest in working on the stage crew with those students over there? We could use some help with painting the sets," Ms. Hodges asked.

"Boy, does that sound like fun," Bennett said, before Owen decided to take advantage of the moment.

"Actually, Ms. Hodges, we wanted to talk to you about a special idea we are working on at our school and could use some help from your *Players*. It's a 'Service Learning' project based on research Bennett and I did on world hunger and hunger in America."

Earlier, as they were walking out the door to take the bus to the high school, Owen remembered to grab his posters and a few of the extra booklets he had prepared for the SG representatives. Once again, in just five minutes, Owen summarized the food drive they were hoping to organize. Now, the director was quietly looking over the materials.

"So you want our thespian troupe to register for a *TOTS-EAT* project, am I correct?"

"Yes," Owen replied, "And we also would like them to go with us on Halloween, to go trick-or-treating with us..."

"...to drive us and help carry the bags of food," Bennett added.

The director was touched by how organized the young children were and how quickly they cut to the chase. "I think this is a great idea. Can you boys stay around; we take a snack break around four and I would like you to discuss this with the troupe."

When Limpho Kane picked up Owen and his friends at the end of rehearsal, she asked, "So, dear children; how did it go today?"

Owen did not know where to begin. "Mom, it was such an amazing day; one thing after another fell into place. First, we got a unanimous vote of approval from the student government. Then we met with Mr. Edney and he loved the project. And this afternoon, we spoke with the *Players* here at the high school and they said they would be "honored"...they really used that word... to work with us. They are going to register the project tomorrow, help us with all the...what was that word, Bennett?"

"'Logistics'...putting everything in place...including driving us on Halloween."

Susie added, "And they are going to give people discounts on the tickets for the play, if they bring a bag of canned goods to the performance they attend. It feels like the *Players* are going to be good partners."

"And they kind of have stopped treating us like babies, don't you think, Susie?" Madeline added.

"I did see a change in the way they spoke with us," Susie said. "Honestly, you did such a good job, Owen.

Your talk was impressive. You pulled this all together in such a brilliant way. You deserve a lot of credit."

Even though he was responding to what Susie had said, he looked at his mother while he spoke. "I appreciate what you said, Susie, but you of all people know this was a group effort. We do make a great team, don't we? And I cannot imagine what my life would be like without all of you in it each and every day. Talk about brothers and sisters; we really are a family!"

As she listened to her son speak, a lump formed in Limpho's throat. She was so moved by her son's love for his friends and the depth of pride they took in his success. She thought back to her conversation with her husband a few nights ago, about Owen changing schools. At the time, she was positive it would be the right thing...but she was wise enough to realize the final decision had to be made by her son.

Now it was Limpho's turn to surprise the children. "I called each of your parents and asked if you could come to our house for dinner and dessert. Given all the attention you have paid to our native homeland, Baruti and I wanted to make you an African meal!"

Susie and Bennett looked at each other and tried to act enthusiastic. Obviously, the Kanes had gone to a lot of trouble to make this meal. However, all they could think about was the horrible gruel they ate when then were on their adventure in Africa.

"What's up with you guys?" Madeline asked, as she saw the strange looks on her friends' faces. "This should be a real treat!"

Little did she know her three friends had witnessed Kigaso eating a huge bug and that they themselves had eaten hot cereal in the middle of a hot afternoon, in the middle of a scorching hot desert. And most likely, she would never know.

The ride back to Owen's home took about ten minutes. When Susie, Bennett, and Madeline entered the Kane house, they were greeted by Owen's little sister Katie and the most deliciously sweet and unusual aroma they had ever smelled. "Welcome to my world," Owen said to his friends.

"Come in, dear children," Limpho said. "Baruti seems to have everything organized. Let's wash up and prepare to give your stomachs a treat."

And what a treat it was! This food was a far cry from what the three friends had experienced in Somalia. Susie turned to Bennett and said, "Remember, we were there in the middle of a famine; people were starving. While these must be native recipes, few, if any of the villagers we met could have possibly prepared such a feast, at least not for many, many years."

The first dish Limpho served was a grain she called *caakiri.* It was made with a tiny, round starch Baruti called *couscous* and had a sauce that Owen said was made from beans, onions, tomato, and curry. Then Limpho brought out a stew made with lamb, potatoes, and the sweetest carrots Susie had ever tasted. This dish had a more spicy sauce than the grain so, to cool their mouths, Limpho also served a cold salad made with cucumbers, mint, and sour cream. But the best part was dessert.

"Oh, wow!" Susie said, as the taste of the sweet fruit filled her mouth. "Are these bananas?" she asked. "They taste a little like the fried bananas we order at Ming Quan."

"Yes, Susie," Limpho told her. "The recipe is called, 'Baked Bananas Gabon', named after the place where it came from. And you are right; it is similar to the Chinese dish you mentioned, only our version is topped with sour cream and brown sugar."

"And what is this amazing treat?" Madeline asked.

It was Owen who answered for his mother. "Those are my favorite! They are 'Pumpkin Fritters'...my mom usually makes them around Halloween when we can buy fresh pumpkins at the store."

"Are these secret family recipes, or could you tell me how to make them?" Susie asked. "My granny is in town and I would love to cook both of them for her."

"How sweet you are, Susie. Of course I will share the recipes with you, dear child. First thing tomorrow morning, before I go to work, I will e-mail them to you. I am flattered that you like my cooking," Limpho said.

The wonderful dinner was over and it was time to make their way home. Even though they could have walked, Baruti insisted on driving the three guests home. What an amazing day this had been. Things were falling into place and the hunger-in-America project was well on its way. With the production of the play the girls were in taking place the week after Halloween, and all the rehearsals that were scheduled, Susie and Madeline were concerned about finding the time to help out with the food drive.

After dropping Madeline off first, they headed to the Gardner home. When they arrived at their house, Susie and Bennett thanked Baruti again for the wonderful dinner and went upstairs to get ready for bed.

Bennett sensed his sister was feeling overwhelmed. So once he finished getting washed, he knocked on the door to her room. Of course, her first reaction when she saw him enter her bedroom was that he wanted to sleep in the other twin bed. But that would not be possible with Granny Ella visiting. However, once Bennett sat down next to her and voiced his suspicions, she was relieved to find out he could appreciate all that lay before her.

"Don't worry, Susie. Owen and I have this covered. You focus on the play, and we will keep the hunger project on course. Just let me know when I can help you along the way. Owen and I are going to work with the *Players* on the scenery, so we'll all be spending a lot of time together at the high school."

That was just fine with Susie. Her brother was growing up right before her eyes and she liked what she saw. He and Owen made a great team and yes, she agreed; Owen really was a part of their family.

CHAPTER EIGHTEEN

A Night to Remember

Saturday evening, October 31, 2009, turned out to be a beautiful night for trick-or-treating. It was warm enough so the children did not have to cover their costumes with jackets and there was no rain to dampen their spirits. All over Merion, teams of high school and elementary students made their ways through the neighborhoods where they had distributed pre-collection cards for the *TOTS-EAT* project.

Right away, Susie, Bennett, Owen, and Madeline could see their planning was paying off. Each of the kids carried a pumpkin-shaped basket with the *TOTS-EAT* logo, just in case some generous homeowner wanted to give them candy as well as food for the hunger project.

At each of the first five houses they went to, at least one bag of canned and packaged goods waited for them. The younger students were so glad to have their high school chaperones, not just to carry the heavy loads, but for their friendship, good cheer, and drive...figuratively and literally, as it was these senior actors who carpooled the elementary students from house to house.

Madeline was especially happy to ride along with the lead in the play; although she would never admit it to anyone, not even her best friend Susie, she had an enormous crush on Johnny Butler. Just the sight of him made her heart skip a beat. She knew he was seven years older than her, but Madeline hoped he would think she was more mature than a typical fifth grader. Although he played the role of her father in the production, she hoped against hope that he might take more than a fatherly interest in her. Well, she could dream, couldn't she? Whenever she could get away with it, Madeline waited in the car with her heartthrob while the others knocked on doors for donations.

Not that he was aware of his fellow student government rep's emotional state that evening, Owen was about to have his own heart-stopping moment in time. They were on Lafayette Road, just down from where the Gardners lived, when Owen was left speechless. They had seen a moving van coming and going the last few days and assumed the new owners of the Hallett house had moved in. Whether or not the new neighbors had gotten the pre-collection card, the children would not know for sure, until they knocked on the door.

As Owen, Bennett, and Susie approached the front porch, they were amazed by the wonderful decorations the homeowners had put up. The house was both spooky and beautiful at the same time. With the full moon lighting his way, Owen walked up to the front door and rang the bell. That was when he almost fainted.

A lovely older woman came to the door. Her white hair was brought up in a bun that rested high on her head. It was not her beauty that first struck Owen, although she certainly was quite lovely. It was her piercing eyes and tiny frame that reminded him of a woman he had only caught a glimpse of...in Somalia. This woman looked just like Audrey Hepburn...an older Audrey Hepburn!

As she placed her bag of donations on the floor by her side, their new neighbor said, "I am so proud of you youngsters. What a wonderful thing you are doing. My husband and I worked as missionaries in many foreign countries over the years; we have seen whole villages of people on the verge of dying from starvation. When I read the card you put in the mailbox, I was so pleased to be able to help our nation's own hungry children. Oh, and here is a little something for the three of you, a little treat," she said, as their new neighbor put a few pieces of candy in each of their pumpkin baskets.

Madeline had stayed with Johnny while her friends accepted this donation. As they walked back to the car, Owen turned to Susie and Bennett and said, "Did you see her? Who did she look like?"

"I noticed it too, Owen," Bennett said. "But you know it wasn't her; Audrey Hepburn died sixteen years ago."

"I know, I know. But I just have to go back and ask her something."

Owen turned and walked back up the steps to the woman's porch. She was still outside, watching the children add her bag to the others in Johnny Butler's car.

"Excuse me...we did not get a chance to meet. My name is Owen Kane; what is your name?"

"Oh, it is nice to meet you, Owen. My name is Andrea Hopkins. My husband Marvin and I moved here from Cincinnati to live closer to our children and grandchildren. On what street do you live?" she asked.

"I live on Revere Road, right around the corner, with my five-year-old sister Katie and our parents. My family moved to America from Somalia when I was four years old. And now this is our homeland."

Owen paused for a minute before asking his next question. "Has anyone ever told you that you look just like Audrey Hepburn, Mrs. Hopkins? You even have the same initials as the star."

"Actually, my dear, yes, I have heard that before. But Miss Hepburn was such an impressive and generous woman, it's hard for me to compare myself in any way to her inner or outer beauty. With that said, my husband has nicknamed me 'Holly Golightly', in honor of Miss Hepburn's character in *Breakfast at Tiffany's*. He too sees the resemblance between the lovely actress and me."

Owen found himself unable to take his eyes off the woman. His brain told him to put his time-travel thoughts away, as there was no way this woman could be the famous actress. But at the same time, he did not want to leave her side.

He was forced to turn and go when Johnny Butler honked the horn. "Owen, come on...we still have two more houses to get to."

"Enjoy the rest of your evening, young man," the woman called out as Owen moved down the steps of her porch for the second time. "And come back to see me again. We should have a visit so I can tell you about our time in Somalia. I have some amazing stories and even some pictures I can show you of your original homeland."

Owen waved and continued toward the waiting car, as he said to himself, "I'm sure you do, Miss Hepburn"... and then caught himself. When he turned one last time, the woman was gone. So he let the moment pass and refocused on what still needed to be done.

There were twenty-six teams of children knocking on doors and gathering bags of donations. After three hours of hard work, Susie and her friends were done with their route. At one point, their high school escort had to stop and call a friend to meet them; they ran out of room for the bags in his car in about two hours. When they arrived back at the high school gym, they unloaded thirty bags from their efforts on behalf of the hungry.

None of the trick-or-treaters were prepared for what they saw as they entered the gymnasium; on every inch of space on the basketball court, from one corner of the room to the other, there were bags and bags of food. Kids high-fived each other and rushed around hugging each team as they arrived at the drop-off.

Both Mr. Edney and Mr. Krug, the high school principal, were trying to count all the bags. In the end, they thought there were 612 of them, all filled to the brim. Although the school did not have a scale large enough to weigh the entire bounty, Mr. Edney weighed one bag, found it to be twenty pounds, and then offered a free ticket to the high school play to the first student who guessed what the approximate total weight would be.

Carl Tracker was the first to shout out, "I know, I know...612 bags times twenty pounds each is 12,240 pounds!"

"Good for you, young man. And here is another ticket for the first person to tell me how many tons that is."

Carol Newman quietly raised her hand and said, "That's about six tons of food!"

"Very good thinking, young lady," Mr. Edney said, as he handed her a ticket.

Mr. Krug's next words almost caused a riot in the gym. "I am so proud of what you have accomplished that the high school is going to give each one of you a ticket to the play next weekend. You won't want to miss seeing your friends Susie Gardner and Madeline Barnett who have starring roles in the production. But be sure you remember to bring your own bag of donations to the performance or you may not be able to get in."

CHAPTER NINETEEN

The Show Will Go On!

With one-half of the hunger project complete, there was still work to be done. It was Tuesday, November 3, and the play was less than a week away. Even though the girls knew their parts backward and forward, they still had to attend the five-hour rehearsals every single day.

And then there was a major setback; Johnny Butler, who played the role of Georg Ludwig von Trapp, had an attack of appendicitis. By the time they got him to the hospital, the infected organ had ruptured, and Johnny was in serious condition. The doctors told the family he would be fine in time, but there was no way he would be able to play his part.

As the director told her anxious cast about the turn of events, she assured them, "Ladies and gentlemen; the show *must* go on! And the show *will* go on. This is why we have understudies."

"What's an 'understudy'?" Owen whispered to Bennett backstage where they were busy painting scenery.

"It's someone who practices a part with the rest of the cast in case something like this happens. That way, the understudy can take over for an actor who cannot perform," Bennett told his friend.

Two days later was the day of the dress rehearsal; this would be the first time Johnny's understudy Steven Foley rehearsed the entire play with the other actors. To everyone's surprise, everything went smoothly. Many members of the cast said Steven might be even better suited for the part. But not Madeline. Every chance she got, she would make comments like, "Oh, Johnny did that soooo much better," or "It's just not the same play without Johnny."

Her friends knew she was just star-struck by the handsome senior. They let her go on, but made sure she kept her voice down so as not to upset their new star.

The first performance was on Friday evening...and it was a packed house. Owen looked out from behind the curtain and was amazed by the sea of people. The auditorium held about a thousand seats, and he could not fine an empty one. The boys knew what this meant; the high school gym must have been filling up with more donations.

The *Players* outdid themselves. By the time the final curtain came down, the audience was on its feet, applauding the director and her talented cast. Every song, every dance step was perfect. No one forgot a line or cue, and the entire cast was grateful Steven Foley had nerves of steel and such a beautiful singing voice. Susie and Madeline could not stop hugging each other; they both felt like stars. And the boys were proud of the contribution they had made to the show's success by working on the sets.

There were two more performances to go; one on Saturday evening and a final matinee on Sunday afternoon. Principal Edney was impressed with the dedication of the *Players*, their willingness to include some of his students in the production, and the enormous collection of bags that stretched from one end of the high school gym to the other.

The previous weekend, Mr. Graham and the Food Cupboard had to make three trips with their truck to get everything over to their warehouse after Halloween. It appeared they would be making twice that many trips by the end of the three performances. Based on the numbers Mr. Edney had used during last week's Halloween collection, he guessed the play brought in at least another ten tons of food for the hungry.

It was a good thing the students did not have school on Monday; their teachers had an in-service day of training. And Tuesday was Election Day, so both the students and teachers had that day to recover from the recent excitement. Once the costumes were put away and the bags of food were locked in the gym, it was time for the cast party.

Ms. Hodges had booked Carlo's Pizza Restaurant for the occasion, and they used some of the money the tickets brought in to pay for all the food the hungry and tired cast and crew would eat.

When everyone arrived at the pizza parlor, Ms. Hodges grabbed a microphone and spoke to the talented group of students. "I am so very proud of each and every one of you. Not only did you put on one of the best performances the *Players* has ever staged, but you did not fold when Johnny became ill, and you supported Steven in his wonderful effort, worked diligently with Merion Elementary students during their food drive, and pulled off the largest charitable event in the history of the school district. The Food Cupboard will give us the final weigh in and, believe it or not, the *ETA* and *ITS* have awards for the hunger projects that are most successful.

"But that is not why we partnered with these smart and talented youngsters you see here tonight. We did this for our community, for those among us who have fallen on tough times, knowing that at any moment, any one of us might need the kindness of others. You are an impressive group of young men and women and it has been my honor to have the privilege of working with you."

The entire cast and crew stood up and cheered for their director. Steven presented her with a bouquet of roses and she surprised everyone by handing out a rose to each member of the cast and production team.

It was a joyful occasion, especially for Madeline. When she got to the restaurant, there was a special person waiting to congratulate his friends; Johnny Butler's parents surprised the cast by bringing him to the party.

Madeline could not do enough for the young man. She waited on him the entire evening. Susie steered her away from where Johnny was seated when his girlfriend, Sarah Groff, walked in the door. Madeline stared daggers at the beautiful girl, wishing with all her might that *she* would 'break-a-leg'.

By this time, all the parents had arrived to take their kids home for a much needed night's sleep. But when Owen saw the Gardners, he rushed over to them and said, "Pleeease, can Bennett and Susie sleep over at my house tonight? I promise we will get right to sleep...no fooling around."

Karen and Eric looked over at the Kanes, who nodded their heads in approval. Since it wasn't a school night, they saw no harm in letting the children celebrate their momentous achievements.

CHAPTER TWENTY

Some Surprising News

By ten o'clock, the three thespians were up in Owen's room, getting ready for bed. The boys were using sleeping bags on the floor, and Susie got the full-sized bed.

When Bennett and Owen went down the hall to get washed, Susie noticed an interesting book sitting on Owen's desk. She had heard of the author, Agatha Christie, and knew the woman was a mystery writer. As she read the back cover of *The Orient Express,* Owen came back into the bedroom and saw her deep in thought. He said, "That's the book I am reading for our next book report. My teacher knows I like mysteries and thought I would relate to Ms. Christie's background."

"What do you mean?" Susie asked.

"Well, you know I have a learning disability, don't you?" Susie nodded and Owen continued. "My teacher told me she had read an article in one of her professional journals that said there were people who suspected Ms. Christie might have also had learning issues. I think it had something to do with her handwriting and spelling skills. Sound like anyone you know, Bennett?" Owen asked, once his friend joined the conversation.

"So, in between my research on Africa, I have also been looking into other famous people who had trouble in school. The school psychologist told me these kinds of problems have nothing to do with how smart you are. Did you know that billionaire Nelson Rockefeller, who was our nation's forty-first vice president under President Gerald Ford, also had trouble with reading and writing? These kinds of learning issues are so much more common than I could ever have imagined. And you know what? When I look back at all we have accomplished since the start of the school year, all the people we are helping, and how much the high school students respected us and our talents, I am feeling a lot more confident."

"Owen, that's great...good for you!" Susie told him.

"Well, maybe not quite so good for me after all. You can't tell anyone this next part. Promise?"

Susie and Bennett did a pinky swear with Owen, and he told them about the conversation he overheard a few months ago when his parents thought he was asleep. "So even though they say it is my choice whether I switch to this new school or not, you know how that goes. If they want me to go there, they will find a way to make sure I make the choice they want."

"Hey, Owen, have you visited the school yet? I don't think your parents would even consider it if they didn't think it could be a good thing for you. And you said it's in Manayunk, right? That is such a cool part of Philly...and only about twenty minutes from here. Maybe you should try to keep an open mind," Bennett gently suggested. "I'll go and take a look at it with you if you want me to."

"Wow, what a great idea! If you would do that for me, I will give it a shot. Honestly, all this after-school tutoring is starting to bug me. I heard my mom say the classes are so small that I would get lots of attention and, speaking of attention, the smaller classes might make it easier for me to concentrate."

"It might give you more time to play with us after school, instead of being cooped up inside doing more and more work just to stay on track. Oh, and by the way, do not think for one minute that you aren't smart. Look how you put this project together. And Madeline told me your speech to the student government was amazingly fabulous. None of us could have done the job you did...and you know how smart we are!"

"That must mean I am smarter than you!"

Bennett had to pause a moment to think about how Owen had turned his words around.

"Not to change the subject, you guys, but this book looks like an exciting murder mystery. Maybe it would make a good bedtime story. Want me to read to you?" Susie asked.

"You know, I also have the book on tape, if you would rather listen to it, Susie. The narrator speaks with a British accent. Did I mention that Agatha Christie was born in Devon, England?"

"Well, I don't mind reading. Speaking of paying attention, I find that when I am listening to someone else read, my mind can start to wander. But if I am reading, well, a book just seems to hold my attention better."

"Mrs. Magen says, "We all learn differently," Owen told his friends. "More and more, I am seeing that is actually true."

Susie asked, "Owen, do you have a flashlight I can use? I don't think your mother would be happy to see your light still on."

Owen kept a flashlight in his closet. He brought it over to where Susie sat and turned off the lamp by the bed. Before she had even picked up the light to begin reading, a beautiful red glow filled every corner of Owen's bedroom. Bennett and Owen looked at each other and, in unison, said, "Take off your shoes!"

Susie did what they asked, agreeing that another possible adventure would be a little too much right now. With that said, she snuggled under the covers with the book propped up in front of her. Susie had probably only finished four pages when she noticed the boys had dozed off. Taking her lead from these young school leaders, she turned off the flashlight and placed it on the floor next to her shoes. That way, if she needed them, Susie would have no trouble finding the special family heirloom. Never again would they leave her side.

Sweet Baked Bananas Gabon

Ingredients:

10 almost-ripe bananas
2 eggs
3 tablespoons of orange juice
1 cup of plain breadcrumbs
1 cup of shredded, sweetened coconut
½ cup of corn oil
1 cup of sour cream
1 cup of brown sugar

Directions: Preheat the oven to 350 degrees Fahrenheit

1. Cut each banana into three pieces, on the diagonal.
2. Beat the eggs with the orange juice.
3. Mix the breadcrumbs with the coconut. Dip the pieces of banana into the combined egg and orange juice, then roll each piece in the crumb mixture and press to coat the banana very well.
4. Sauté the bananas in the oil until they are slightly brown all over.
5. Drain them on paper towels and then place the pieces on a non-stick cookie sheet.
6. Bake the pieces in the oven for about 7 minutes.
7. Place three pieces of banana in a glass dessert dish and top each serving with 2 tablespoons of sour cream and 1 tablespoon of brown sugar.

Makes 10 servings

Somali Pumpkin Fritters

Ingredients:

2 cups of fresh-cooked pumpkin meat (you can use canned pumpkin, but fresh tastes better)
1 egg, beaten
3 tablespoons of flour
1 teaspoon of cinnamon
1 teaspoon of baking powder
1 tablespoon of sugar
1 teaspoon of lemon juice
1 cup of corn oil
1 cup of brown sugar
1 pint of ice cream (any flavor you like)

1. Buy a fresh pumpkin, cut it open, scrape out the seeds, and remove the meat from the shell. Bake in a 350-Fahrenheit-degree oven until the meat is soft. Mash well and then drain off any excess liquid that may have accumulated.
2. Combine the pumpkin, egg, flour, cinnamon, baking powder, sugar, and lemon juice. Mix well.
3. Heat the oil in an 8-inch deep pan until it is very hot, but not burning. Then drop the fritter mixture by heaping tablespoons into the oil. Fry the fritters until they are golden brown and drain them on paper towels before serving.
4. Place the fritters on a serving platter and sprinkle them with brown sugar. Serve with a scoop of ice cream!

Makes 6 servings

Welcome to the Susie's Shoesies Book Club!

You may have noticed that when you see a book for the first time, you often have questions before you even start reading. Sometimes the cover will give you clues about who the characters are and what may happen to them in the book. If you look at the *Before Reading* questions when you are ready to begin a chapter, they will give you some additional ideas of what Susie and Bennett might be up to.

Once you start reading, you will learn more about the adventure that lies ahead. Take a look at the *During Reading* questions for each chapter and they will help you predict what might happen next. When you have finished reading a chapter, the *After Reading* questions can help you tie everything that happened in the chapter together. But be careful; make sure you have read a few pages of a chapter before you look at the *During Reading* questions, and you should have finished a chapter before discussing the *After Reading* questions. If you get ahead of yourself, you may ruin surprises that are about to be revealed.

To get the most out of the Susie's Shoesies experience, before you begin to read, you and your friends or family should make one of Susie's special desserts. Then pour yourself a glass of cold milk, or heat up some hot chocolate, and enjoy the journey back in time.

Many schools are using the Susie's Shoesies series to help their students learn about historic events and understand difficult social issues. While children across the country are discussing the questions that go with each chapter in their classrooms, many readers are reading the books by themselves, sitting in bed or in a cushy chair, as they travel back in time with Susie and Bennett.

Whether you are reading the books for school or just for the fun of it, by going to www.SusiesShoesies.com, you can find out about the new book club that will be starting in November 2012. Although we are still working out the details and kinks, we will most likely use Skype to talk to each other. Here is how we think it will work.

Once a month, I will post two questions on the Susie's Shoesies website; the chapters the questions refer to will be listed, as well as the procedure you will need to use for me to add you to a group Skype call. I will list the date and time of the group call, and you will need to confirm if you are attending through the website e-mail. Of course, you will need a camera and speakers for your computer.

In the next few months, we will finalize the procedure and post more specific directions on the web. So, be patient, keep reading, and we will meet before you know it. By the way, we can also do a book club Skype with your classroom. Talk to your teacher and have her contact me through the website.

If you or your teacher or friends post a question to me when I am traveling to do a book reading and signing, it may take me a while to respond. You can check on the web to see where my next appearance will be... and I hope to meet you at one of these events, or via Skype, soon.

In friendship,
Sue Levine

Book Club Discussion Questions
Prologue: What kind of dream is this?

Before Reading
1. When you look at the cover of this book, what do you think Susie, Bennett, and their friend Owen are doing?
2. Why are they dressed the way they are?
3. What does, 'Trick or Treat so Kids Can Eat' mean?
4. To what country do you think the kids will travel?
5. Do you know the names of any famous people who went there?
6. What does the title of this book make you think the story is about?

During Reading
1. Where is Somalia?
2. What movie star do the children think they will meet?
3. Why do famous people get involved in charity organizations?

After Reading
1. Why did the older woman tell the children not to speak?
2. To what town are they headed?
3. Think of two possible ways the kids might be having the experience they are.

Book Club Discussion Questions

Chapter One: A Tough School Year for Owen

Before Reading

1. Why is Owen so interested in Somalia?
2. What prize did Owen and Bennett win last school year?
3. Does your school have a student government and, if they do, would you like to be involved in that organization? Why or why not?
4. About whom was the last report you wrote in school?
5. Have you ever done any work for a charity and, if so, what did you accomplish?

During Reading

1. How did Miss Hepburn feel about what she saw in Somalia?
2. What do you think 'food insecurity' means?
3. What are some of the effects starvation can have on a child's future?
4. What kind of learning problems was Owen having?

After Reading

1. Do you have any learning problems and, if so, how do they affect your school work?
2. Do you think Owen's life in Somalia had anything to do with his learning issues?
3. Can a person be very smart and still have a learning disorder and, if so, how is that possible?
4. If you are worried about something, how can that affect your learning?

Book Club Discussion Questions
Chapter Two: Where Did I Come From?

Before Reading
1. In what country, state, and city were you born?
2. Have you ever met a famous actor or sports star and, if so, where?
3. Have you ever had a tutor and, if so, what kinds of things did that person help you with?
4. What do you know about hunger and starvation?

During Reading
1. What was Katie Kane worried about, and why?
2. Are there any people who are starving in America and, if so, what are communities doing to help them?
3. On what continent is Somalia located?

After Reading
1. Do you think it was a good idea to take older students in Somalia out of school to teach younger children to read and write?
2. How did charities provide food and supplies to the starving people of Africa?
3. What natural disaster caused the Kane family to leave their homeland?

Book Club Discussion Questions
Chapter Three: Susie Tells Owen

Before Reading
1. Have you ever been bullied and, if so, how did it make you feel?
2. If one of your friends told you she had magical shoes, would you believe her?
3. Have you ever been to a country during a war? What do you think that would be like?

During Reading
1. How did the older woman think the man who was left in the desert might be saved?
2. Why do the rebels behave the way they do?
3. What did Susie's mother give her for her ninth birthday, and what might that gift have to do with the current adventure?

After Reading
1. How did Owen happen to know what a *shaman* is?
2. Why did Owen ask his friend Bennett to "Pinch me"?
3. How do you think the kids will get home at the end of their adventure?

Book Club Discussion Questions
Chapter Four: Are We There Yet?

Before Reading
1. What kind of clothes do the village people in Somalia wear?
2. What kind of food do the village people in Somalia eat?
3. What is a 'refugee'? What is a 'relocation camp'?

During Reading
1. Why did Kagiso cover the children's heads with her scarf?
2. Why did the villagers not complain about their lack of food and water?
3. What was Kagiso hoping to accomplish by shoving one of the soldiers?

After Reading
1. Why do you think the soldier's daughter wanted Susie's shoes?
2. Why do you think Kagiso told Susie not to say a word?
3. About how many years had the shoes been in Susie's family, and how did you arrive at that number?
4. What do you think will happen when the little girl puts on Susie's shoes?

Book Club Discussion Questions
Chapter Five: Good News from Above

Before Reading
1. Do you remember what you thought when you saw your first airplane?
2. If you were able to travel back in time, would you tell your friends about it? Why or why not?
3. Have you ever been somewhere and thought you saw someone who looked a lot like someone else you knew? When and where did this happen?

During Reading
1. Why did Susie and Bennett tell Owen not to tell the people from the village what he knew about Audrey Hepburn?
2. Should the kids tell the villagers about the 2004 tsunami? Why or why not?

After Reading
1. Who do you think the young man and woman were that Owen saw as he was leaving the camp on the truck?
2. What do you think the name 'Kagiso' means?
3. Where do you think Susie, Bennett, and Owen are going?

Book Club Discussion Questions
Chapter Six: A Star in the Evening Sky

Before Reading
1. What is a feeding station, and what kinds of people are sent there?
2. Have you ever seen an award-winning actor in a play and, if so, who, and what play did you see?
3. What does the flag of the United Nations look like?

During Reading
1. What town had the children and villagers traveled to, and does that town still exist today?
2. What does the name '*UNICEF*' stand for, and what do you know about that organization?3. What do you know about '*CARE*' and the '*Red Cross*'?

After Reading
1. Now that Susie's shoes are gone, how do you think the kids will get home?
2. Why did Bennett think it might have been a good idea that they did not get to meet Miss Hepburn?
3. What did Susie try to explain to Kagiso when the woman was sad and thought she did not get to see a show?

Book Club Discussion Questions
Chapter Seven: Who's Afraid of the Dark?

Before Reading
1. If you were forced to sleep on the hard ground, what might you do to make a bed for yourself?
2. How long do you think the kids will stay in Somalia? Why?
3. Why do you think Susie, Bennett, and Owen ended up in Somalia?
4. Do you think Susie has any doubts about their being able to return to Merion?

During Reading
1. How does Owen think Susie and Bennett got back from Sweden, and why?
2. What happens when Susie takes off her shoes?
3. Why did Susie have a lump in her throat?

After Reading
1. What does it mean to "put on a brave face"?
2. What do you think Susie's granny would say if she found out the shoes were gone?
3. Have you ever lost or broken something that was very important to your family and, if so, what was it, and how did they react when you told them what happened?

Book Club Discussion Questions
Chapter Eight: Oh, to Be
Back Home in my Own Bed

Before Reading
1. What kinds of birds live in your backyard?
2. Do you have a wind chime outside your house and, if so, do you enjoy the sounds it makes?
3. What does the term 'self-pity' mean?

During Reading
1. Why were Susie's feet so dirty, and what could this mean?
2. Why did Susie start to cry when she woke up?
3. What did Susie find on the floor by the side of her bed, and how did they get there?

After Reading
1. What led Bennett to believe Susie had her shoes back?
2. When Karen Gardner saw her daughter had her shoes on so early in the morning, what did she think had happened?
3. How did the kids know what Mrs. Gardner had been baking?
4. Why did Susie want to call her granny, even though she was coming to visit the next day?

Book Club Discussion Questions
Chapter Nine: Help from Granny Ella

Before Reading
1. When was the last time you called one of your grandparents?
2. What year was it now that Susie was home again?
3. How many years back in time had Susie, Bennett, and Owen traveled when they thought they had been to Somalia?
4. Do you think Kagiso is still alive? Why or why not?
5. What is a 'conservatory'?

During Reading
1. What was the good news Susie was looking forward to telling her grandmother?
2. What does Kagiso's name mean, and when Susie found that out, how did it make her feel?
3. How was it that Granny Ella once lost her shoes?

After Reading
1. How did Susie's grandmother get her shoes back?
2. Who told Granny Ella the background of the red shoes?
3. Why did Susie think the shoes "carried with them a much larger responsibility"?

Book Club Discussion Questions
Chapter Ten: Back to Reality

Before Reading
1. Have you ever heard about or read a book called, *A River Runs Through It?* If so, did you enjoy it?
2. Have you ever waited till the last moment to complete a school project and, if so, what did that feel like?
3. Who helps you when you are having trouble with a school assignment?
4. If you were going to write a story about your life with one of your brothers or sisters, what would be the first thing you would want to tell your readers?

During Reading
1. What was different about the two brothers in the book Owen had read, and in what ways were they alike?
2. Why did Owen use a 'story web', and have you ever used one with your own writing?
3. Do you prefer to write stories or reports and why?
4. Have you ever used a 'spell-check' feature on a computer and, if so, was that helpful? How can that type of software still leave words misspelled?

After Reading
1. Do you think the Academy In Manayunk might be a good school for Owen? Why or why not?
2. Why did Owen think he could handle the situation he overheard his parents talking about?

Book Club Discussion Questions
Chapter Eleven: Is a New Star About to Be Born?

Before Reading
1. Have you ever been called to the office over the PA system at your school and, if so, how did it make you feel?
2. If you could win a free trip, to where would you want to go, and why?
3. Do you feel like you have a good relationship with your principal and, if so, why?
4. What is a 'permission form' and have you ever needed your parents to sign one?

During Reading
1. Why was Madeline surprised to hear that Susie had been traveling?
2. If you were asked to be an actor in one of your town's high school plays, would you want to do it? Why or why not?
3. What does the word 'thespian' mean?

After Reading
1. How hard would it be for you to have play rehearsals every day after school and still keep up with your homework?
2. Have you ever heard the expression 'break-a-leg' before and, if so, when was that, and what did it make you think?

Book Club Discussion Questions
Chapter Twelve: Rhyming is Not Such a Bad Thing

Before Reading
1. Have you ever used a rhyming phrase as the title to something you wrote and, if so, when, and for what project?
2. What is your favorite snack food?
3. Does your mother work outside your home and, if so, what does she do?

During Reading
1. Why does Owen get to have his own computer?
2. Is there a difference between hunger in America and hunger in Africa and, if so, how would you describe it?
3. Why does Owen leave his classroom when he has a test?

After Reading
1. Before you use a slogan or title for a project, name two reasons it is good idea to 'search' the name prior to using it?
2. What was the 'Food Cupboard'? Do you have one in your neighborhood, and have you ever been there?
3. Does your high school have an *International Thespian Society* troupe?

Book Club Discussion Questions

Chapter Thirteen: I Can Already Taste the Cake!

Before Reading
1. What is your favorite kind of cake?
2. When was the last time one of your grandparents came to visit?
3. What is the most special present you ever got from one of your grandparents?
4. Does your school have a 'chorus' and, if so, are you a member of it?

During Reading
1. What and who was waiting for Susie when she got home from school?
2. How did Granny Ella know about Susie's adventure in Africa?
3. How did Susie's mother know so much about the red shoes?
4. Who gave Susie's grandmother the red shoes and why?

After Reading
1. Even if the shoes are not magical, what makes them so special?
2. Do you have any family heirlooms that you know of?
3. Name all the people who know, at this point, about the shoes and the powers they may possess.

Book Club Discussion Questions
Chapter Fourteen: More Research

Before Reading
1. What the last thing you 'searched' something online?
2. What do you know about 'organizations' and 'charters'?
3. Does your family get any professional magazines on a regular basis and, if so, which ones?

During Reading
1. What does TTS software make possible?
2. Does your school use any writing software to help assist the students?
3. Do you have a drama teacher at your school?

After Reading
1. If your school put on a play, would you want to be in it? Why or why not?
2. Do you think your school might want to do a *TOTS-EAT* project? Why or why not?
3. What is a 'press release'?

Book Club Discussion Questions
Chapter Fifteen: A Team Approach

Before Reading
1. What does the term 'team approach' mean?
2. How late into the morning do you usually sleep on the weekends?
3. Have you ever seen the play or movie version of *The Sound of Music* and, if so, did you enjoy it?
4. What is a 'partnership'?

During Reading
1. Why did the boys initially think it was "very, very cool" that the girls were going to be in the high school play?
2. What did the high school play have to do with their *TOTS-EAT* project?
3. Why did the kids hope the high school *Players* would drive them around when they went trick-or-treating?

After Reading
1. About how many pounds of food were donated to the *TOTS-EAT* program in 2009?
2. Why did Susie decide they should put off telling the *Players* about their hunger project for a few days?
3. Do you think the high school students will want to get involved in the elementary school hunger project? Why or why not?

Book Club Discussion Questions
Chapter Sixteen: Is Everyone on Board?

Before Reading
1. What is the name of your local newspaper? Have they ever mentioned you or your family in an article and, if so, what did they write about?
2. What costume did you wear last Halloween?
3. Have you ever gone to your principal for help and, if so, for what did you need his/her assistance?

During Reading
1. Why did Owen prepare posters for the student government meeting?
2. Why did the children need their principal's permission to get involved in the hunger project?

After Reading
1. Why did the SG members look so sad when they left the meeting?
2. What "sealed the deal" with the representatives?
3. What was so interesting about Susie using the word 'dramatic' when she referred to the *Players*?

Book Club Discussion Questions

Chapter Seventeen: Playing Ball with the Big Guys

Before Reading
1. What does the title of this chapter make you think the next few pages are about?
2. Have you ever gotten lost in a large building, unable to find where you needed to go?
3. What does the word 'logistics' mean?

During Reading
1. What grade are Owen and Bennett in? Susie and Madeline?
2. In what country does *The Sound of Music* take place?
3. Why did Owen bring his posters and booklet to his meeting with Ms. Hodges?

After Reading
1. What does the word 'unanimous' mean, and why did that kind of SG vote make Owen so happy?
2. Why did Susie say that Owen deserved "a lot of the credit"?
3. Have you ever eaten African food and, if so, what did you have? Did you enjoy it?
4. Which of the two desserts sounded the yummiest to you? Do you think you might make one of them for your family?

Book Club Discussion Questions
Chapter Eighteen: A Night to Remember

Before Reading

1. What do the words 'figuratively' and 'literally' mean?
2. Can you remember any of your neighbors decorating their houses for Halloween in an amazing way? What did they use to make their homes look so special?
3. If you are trick-or-treating for a donation to a charity, do you think the homeowners should also hand out candy? Why or why not?

During Reading

1. What was it about his new neighbor that made Owen think of Audrey Hepburn?
2. From what state had Mrs. Hopkins recently moved?
3. Had Marvin and Andrea Hopkins ever been to Somalia and, if so, what do you think they were doing there?

After Reading

1. Do you think Owen will go back and visit his new neighbors again and, if so, why or why not?
2. How many pounds are there in a ton?
3. If one hundred schools across the country do what the students from Merion Elementary did, how many tons of food would they collect?

Book Club Discussion Questions
Chapter Nineteen: The Show Will Go On!

Before Reading
1. What does the word 'understudy' mean? Have you ever seen a play where an understudy took the place of another actor? How well did you think the understudy performed?
2. What do you think most people's first reaction is when they hear there will be an understudy performing?
3. What does the crew of a play do? Do they play an important role in a production? Would you like to be a member of a stage crew?
4. What is a 'teacher in-service day'?

During Reading
1. Was Steven Foley a talented performer and, if so, what makes you think that?
2. How did the donations get to the Food Cupboard?
3. How much more food was collected from the performances?
4. Do you think it is a good idea to ask people to bring a donation to a play or religious event? Why or why not?

After Reading
1. Why do you think Johnny Butler came to the cast party?
2. Why did Owen want Bennett and Susie to sleep over at his house?
3. Why did Madeline want Sarah Groff to 'break-a-leg', and did she really mean for the girl to be injured?

Book Club Discussion Questions

Chapter Twenty: Some Surprising News

Before Reading

1. What do you know about Agatha Christie?
2. Who was Nelson Rockefeller?
3. What is a professional journal?
4. Have you ever heard of a famous person who also had learning issues and, if so, who?
5. Do any of your friends get support for learning issues at school and, if so, what kind of help do they get? Do you think that is a good thing? Why or why not?

During Reading

1. Have you ever been to a special school for children who learn differently and, if so, what did you think of their program?
2. How is it possible for someone to be very smart and yet still have learning issues?
3. Have you ever had trouble paying attention when you were reading something and, if so, when?

After Reading

4. Do you think Owen should stay at Merion Elementary or go to the Academy In Manayunk? Why do you feel the way you do?
5. Why did Owen and Bennett tell Susie to "Take off your shoes!"?
6. To what country do you think the children will travel to in the next Susie's Shoesies adventure? Why?

Read More about It

Whether or not you believe this book is about a realistic dream the characters all have on the same night, or you think they went on a real and mysterious time-travel adventure, will affect whether you think Susie, Bennett, and Owen actually saw Audrey Hepburn when she appeared in Somalia in 1992. Although there is no historical evidence to support that the children were there, this book is historically accurate, to the best of the author's ability, regarding Miss Hepburn's heroic contributions to world hunger and the history of Somalia. The content relates to the historic elements of Miss Hepburn's life and her part in the history of *UNICEF*; they are biographic in nature and correct and accurate, to the best of the author's ability.

The information regarding the *Educational Theatre Association*, the *International Thespian Society*, and *TOTS-EAT* is historically accurate, to the best of the author's ability. The author has a working relationship with these organizations and is so impressed with their efforts and the manner in which their history and goals align with the story she is telling that she is donating ten percent of her royalties from **Susie's Shoesies...The Show Must Go On!** to the *ETA*.

Read More about It

Book, Article, and Play References

Cardillo, M. 2011. *Just Being Audrey*. New York: Balzer & Bray, an imprint of Harper Collins Publishers.

Christie, A. 2011 (first published 1934). *Murder on the Orient Express*. New York: HarperCollins Publishers.

Ferrer, S. H. 2003. *Audrey Hepburn, an Elegant Spirit: A Son Remembers*. New York: Atria Books, a division of Simon and Schuster, Inc.

Hellstern, M. 2004. *How to Be Lovely: The Audrey Hepburn Way of Life*. New York: Dutton.

Maclean, N. 2001. *A River Runs Through It and Other Stories*. Chicago: University of Chicago Press.

Rice, D. 2008. *Audrey Hepburn*. Essex, England: Pearson Education Limited.

Siegel, L. S. 1988. "Agatha Christie's Learning Disability." *Canadian Psychology/Psychologie canadienne* 29(2):213–216.

The Sound of Music. By Lindsay, H. and Crouse, R. Directed by C. Hickman, C., Lunt-Fontanne Theater, New York, NY, November 16, 1959.

Web Publications

"Agatha Christie." *Wikipedia.* Retrieved May 22, 2012, http://en. Wikipedia.org/wiki/Agatha_Christie

"Audrey Hepburn...A Tribute to her Humanitarian Work." *Educational Broadcasting-The MacNeil/Lehrer NewsHour, November 5, 1992.* Transcript retrieved December 8, 2011, http://www.ahepburn.com/interview5.html

"Audrey Hepburn." *Gale Encyclopedia of Biography.* Retrieved December 19, 2011, http://www.answers.com/topic/audrey-hepburn

"Audrey Hepburn." *Wikipedia.* Retrieved May 29, 2011, http://en.wikipedia.org/wiki/Audrey_Hepburn

"Audrey Hepburn's UNICEF Field Missions." Retrieved March 2, 2012, http://www.audrey1.org

"Hunger Facts." *Educational Theatre Association.* Retrieved June 12, 2012, http://schooltheatre.org/society/programs/tots/forms

"Profile: Audrey Hepburn, UNICEF Goodwill Ambassador." Retrieved June 12, 2012, www.unicef.org/about/history/.../audrey_hepburn.../doc401478.PDF

"Puntland." *Wikepedia.* Retrieved May 16, 2012, http://en.wikipedia.org/Wiki/Puntland

"South African Names." Retrieved May 14, 2012, http://babynamesworld.parentsconnect.com/category-south-african-names.html

"Somalia." *World Vision.* Retrieved March 2, 2012, http://www.Worldvision.org

"Somalia." Retrieved May 14, 2012, http://www.every-culture.com/Sa-Th/Somalia.html

About the Author

Sue Madway Levine has been working with children, families, and schools for more than forty years. As a speech and language therapist, a learning disabilities resource teacher, a college professor, a researcher, and a published author, Sue has dedicated her professional life to making a positive difference in the field of education.

During her work at Dominican University in San Rafael, California, Sue hosted game-making workshops for local teachers. This led to her working in the toy and game industry, inventing new products for companies such as Parker Brothers, Milton Bradley, Hasbro, Mattel, Pressman Toy Company, Tiger Electronics, and The Great American Puzzle Factory. After having two of her textbooks published by Academic Therapy Publishing, Sue has now turned to writing children's literature.

Presently, she is in private practice as the Director of Educational Services for The Child and Family Study Team. She lives in a suburb of Philadelphia, Pennsylvania, with her husband, a service learning coordinator at a local school district. Sue spends her free time reading, gardening, making 'Sailor's Valentines', and traveling. If you would like more information about Sue or *Susie's Shoesies*, such as watching chapter readings, following Sue as she meets children across the country, or a chewy, gooey, dark chocolate fudge cake cooking lesson, go to *www.SusiesShoesies.com*.

Look for the next book in this exciting adventure series, *Susie's Shoesies... The Mystery Inside the Mystery!* in book stores everywhere, summer 2013.